heart to heart

Lurlene McDaniel

heart to heart

DELACORTE PRESS

Copyright © 2010 by Lurlene McDaniel

All rights reserved. Published by Delacorte Press, an imprint of Random House Children's Books, a division of Random House, Inc., New York.

Delacorte Press is a registered trademark and the colophon is a trademark of Random House, Inc.

Scripture quotations marked (NIV) are from the Holy Bible, New International Version. Copyright © 1973, 1978, 1984 by International Bible Society. Used by permission of Zondervan Bible Publishers.

Visit us on the Web! www.randomhouse.com/teens

Educators and librarians, for a variety of teaching tools, visit us at www.randomhouse.com/teachers

Library of Congress Cataloging-in-Publication Data
McDaniel, Lurlene.
  Heart to heart / Lurlene McDaniel. — 1st ed.   p. cm.
  Summary: Relates the complicated friendship of a teenaged girl, her best friend, her best friend's boyfriend, and a young heart transplant recipient.
  ISBN 978-0-385-73460-8 (hc) — ISBN 978-0-385-90459-9 (glb)
  ISBN 978-0-375-89652-1 (e-book)
  [1. Friendship—Fiction. 2. Death—Fiction. 3. Heart—Transplantation—Fiction. 4. Fathers and daughters—Fiction.]
  I. Title.
PZ7.M4784172He 2010   [Fic]—dc22   2009017343

The text of this book is set in 11-point Adobe Garamond.
Printed in the United States of America
10 9 8 7 6 5 4 3 2 1
First Edition

This book is dedicated to Lois and to Kaitlyn,
whose heart lives on.

The last enemy to be destroyed is death.
1 Corinthians 15:26 (NIV)

A Note from the Author

The name Elowyn is unusual, but I've loved it from the first time I heard it. The name belongs to the daughter of a friend of mine, and I was told that my friend and her husband "made it up" after reading Tolkien's Lord of the Rings trilogy. No matter. In fact, it is a real name in the Cornish tradition and means "strong elm"—as in elm tree. Origins of names are quite varied. It's fascinating to learn why you were given your name and then to investigate its roots. You might want to do a Web search for *your* name and see what you find out.

This story is fictional, but the phenomenon of "cellular memory" has been recorded by organ transplant recipients on numerous occasions, especially in cases of heart transplants. It is the idea that all human cells can store memories of the body and these memories can be passed along through an organ transplant. Medical science has proven that only the brain can store a memory, and most scientists believe that cellular memory is only speculative. And yet reports persist from many transplant recipients about how they assumed certain personality traits, likes, and dislikes after their transplants. I found this intriguing and used the idea in this novel.

part one

· 1 ·

Kassey

Elowyn Eden and I became best friends.

We met the summer before were were going into seventh grade, when we were hospital roommates in the orthopedic wing, waiting for the same surgeon to fix broken bones. I'd busted up my arm playing volleyball (my favorite sport), and Elowyn had done a number on her left leg skating. She asked me, "Are you scared?"

"About the operation? Not a bit," I said, then dropped my water pitcher because my hands were shaking so much I couldn't pour water into a cup. The pitcher splatted on the floor, and after we watched the water spread everywhere, Elowyn raised an imaginary microphone and said, "Cleanup on aisle four."

We started laughing and couldn't stop. Hours later, we'd talked ourselves hoarse, only stopping long enough to eat dinner. Elowyn and her parents had just moved from South Carolina to Alpharetta, a suburb of Atlanta and my hometown since Mom and Dad split when I was three. Turned out Elowyn lived in a gated garden-home community five blocks over from our house. "So tell me what I'm facing at my new school," she demanded.

We were going to be in the same middle school, so I gave her an earful about who was who and what was what of the kids I knew would be our classmates. She took notes on a hospital napkin. That was so Elowyn—she made lists and took notes like nobody I'd ever met. By the time we left the hospital, we were each wearing a cast signed with the other's name and phone number. She called first, and because I was more mobile than she was, Mom took me to her house a few days later.

Her room was awesome! Her mother—"Call me Terri, *not* Mrs. Eden," she insisted with a smile—was an artsy-craftsy type, and the whole house looked like something out of a decorating magazine, with lots of bright walls and piles of pretty pillows. Elowyn's room had hand-painted vines and fields of flowers growing up the walls. The room was blue and yellow, the flowers pale purple. My house was beige; my room seemed dreary. I'd hung posters, but the space was quite bland.

"It's supposed to be the French countryside," Elowyn said. "France is my favorite place in the world. So romantic. I'm going to Paris on my honeymoon."

"Are you getting married anytime soon?" I joked.

"Someday . . . and he'll be so handsome. Maybe I'll meet a French exchange student and marry him."

I hadn't thought about getting married to anybody, much less someone from a particular country. I walked to the wall and touched the painted flowers. They looked so real. "What kind of flowers?"

"Lavender. Can't you just see whole fields of it? And I love the way it smells. It's my favorite perfume." She spritzed the air with a bottle from her dresser, and the scent was wonderful.

Elowyn seemed so grown-up to me. I didn't have a special fragrance except for the strawberry-scented shampoo I used. I kept looking around her perfect bedroom. "Your mom's talented."

"That's true. She's one of a kind, but it's my daddy who understands me best."

Elowyn's dad was a lawyer, a Southern man who said goofy things like "Don't get off the porch if you can't run with the big dogs" and "Wake up and smell the coffee." I didn't get the point of most of his sayings, but one thing I did get: Elowyn had him wrapped around her little finger. He called her Sugar Plum. I admit, the one thing I ever envied about Elowyn was her relationship with her dad, because I'd grown up with mine long gone.

My mom was a claims adjuster for a huge insurance company and worked long hours, so we were both happy when I fell in with Elowyn and had someplace to hang. I'd grown up with Mom working and me going to day care. No biggie. When I turned twelve, I got to come straight home from school and stay by myself doing homework and watching TV. I liked being around Elowyn and her family—so much like the families I saw on old television shows. Terri always met us at the door, and was always working on some project—gourmet cooking, painting watercolor landscapes. Elowyn and I traded books we loved, and after our casts came off, we parked ourselves at the community pool, turning our bodies buttery tan and swimming to rebuild our shriveled limbs.

In seventh grade, I lured her into volleyball, and between us we played a wicked game. Elowyn was left-handed, so few people on opposing teams could return her hook ball. I was a power server. The coaches loved us.

We took up another habit the summer between seventh and eighth grades.

"How'd you like to come on our family vacation?" she asked me.

"Vacation?"

"A trip."

"I know what a vacation is." Mom and I rarely took vacations. If we traveled it was to see Grandma and Grandpa in Michigan. Talk about a long drive! Otherwise, we just stayed home, because Mom was tired and because vacations cost money we didn't have.

Elowyn sat with a bounce on her bed. "Do you know what it's like to be trapped for a week with my family doing tourist stuff somewhere I don't want to go to in the first place?"

"No idea," I said, but thinking, *Lucky you!*

"*B-o-r-i-n-g.* Anyway, I got this idea that if I took a friend with me, I'd have a lot more fun than just hanging with Mom and Dad."

"You have fun parents."

She rolled her eyes. "Oh sure. We run around, but we never go anyplace cool."

I didn't get it.

"So," she went on, "I asked Mom if I could bring you along."

"You want me to come?"

"You're my best friend."

"And you're mine."

"Then it makes sense, don't you think? We'll have a ball doing things together, and Mom and Dad will have each other and they won't feel like they have to keep me entertained. It'll be a blast!"

"I—I don't know if Mom will let me. . . ."

She held up her hand. "My mom will handle it."

And Terri did handle it. In August, I went with Elowyn and her parents to Destin, Florida, to a beach house they rented overlooking the ocean on sugary white sand. Elowyn's parents played golf and we lounged on the beach flirting with cute guys. Between eighth and ninth grades, I went with them to a resort in Hilton Head, South Carolina, where Elowyn and I caught the interest of two guys who said they were in college. We sneaked out of our room adjoining her parents' and met the guys by the pool in the moonlight. My guy, Todd, kissed me until my head spun and my blood ran hot. It was all new to me. Then he decided to put his hand inside my top. I jerked away. "Don't!"

"Why not?" His voice was not nice.

Shivers of excitement shot through me, but I pulled away. "I—I said no, so it's no."

"What are you? Some lousy tease?" His face, so handsome and romantic in the light of the moon, turned snarly.

I shoved hard and he went backward into the pool. "Let's go!" I cried to Elowyn, and she broke free of an embrace from her guy and ran with me for the pool gate and the patio door to our room, which we'd left unlocked. The guys called us some names but they didn't follow.

We locked the door and fell back on the bed, breathing hard. I was scared. Elowyn was laughing. "Wow!"

"Shhh!" I said. "Don't wake your folks."

"Never happen." She raised herself up on her elbows. "Why'd you run?"

I told her.

"You know guys want to do more if you start kissing them."

"Not without permission. Don't you agree?"

"Older guys especially expect stuff. You know that."

My face got hot.

"It's okay," she said. "We'll never see them again anyway."

"You think?"

"Positive. What guy wants to be with a girl who almost drowns him?"

We dissolved into a fit of giggles.

In ninth grade, we entered Alpha High School, a place so large we needed maps to find our way around the buildings. Fortunately we made the junior varsity volleyball team, which gave us a leg up in the dog-eat-dog world of incoming freshmen. Once the team started winning, people began to know who we were. Not a bad place to be. And then, with little warning, my cozy little world shifted.

Elowyn got a boyfriend.

· 2 ·

Kassey

The boy was Wyatt Nolan, a ninth grader with curly brown hair and dark brown eyes. Elowyn pointed him out to me on the basketball court in February during a game where we were sitting in the bleachers cheering for our team. "What do you think of him?" she asked over the noise of the crowd.

He was a purple and gold blur running down-court. "I can't see his face."

"It's gorgeous," she said. "Don't you think he looks French?"

"I don't know. What difference does it make?"

"He's in my French class."

"Okay. Does that make him more adorable?"

She tilted her chin at me and smiled. "It does."

She hooked him. By the end of basketball season,

she was wearing his JV jacket and they were texting each other ten times a day. Not that cells are allowed at Alpha, but she managed to communicate with him. She and Wyatt were inseparable. Which meant I got shoved aside. Okay, maybe not *shoved,* but I definitely took a backseat in her life priorities. Elowyn was immersed in this guy. At first, I moped around feeling sorry for myself. When your best friend gets all preoccupied with "love" and there's no room for anyone else, your feelings get hurt.

Our friendship caught a break the summer between our freshman and sophomore years because Wyatt went to basketball camp, then to Indiana to visit his grandparents. I didn't miss him. Elowyn did. Her family's "vacation" was to Clearwater, Florida, and I was invited—just like old times. I was ready to have fun, but Elowyn dragged around halfheartedly. I couldn't even lure her into the ice cream parlor for her favorite comfort food, Chunky Monkey. The girl had a bodacious sweet tooth. "I'm buying," I said. "Waffle cones and toppings!" All she talked about was how much she missed Wyatt.

When I mentioned it, she went off on me. "You don't know what it's like to be in love."

I kept my thoughts to myself.

"You should get a boyfriend."

"No one I like," I said. It was true. Guys our age at Alpha seemed immature to me. Deep down, I felt shy about guys. I never had a dad around to talk to. Men were not really part of my life.

Elowyn and Wyatt talked on their cells for an hour every night while I watched TV or lay on the bed tossing a volleyball into the air endlessly. If they were still attached to each other next summer, I told myself I was staying home instead of going on her vacation.

Once we got home, Elowyn and I went back-to-school shopping and that was fun. She had a calendar on her bedroom wall with the days marked off until Wyatt returned. "What's this?" I asked the first time I saw it. "I used to mark the days before Christmas off when I was a kid, but I outgrew it."

She stuck out her tongue. "Don't be mean."

When school started, Elowyn and Wyatt were again joined at the hip and I was left to figure out my life on my own. They never really included me and I didn't want to be a tagalong anyway. But a few months into the new school year, cracks started to form in their "love."

"I hate him!" Elowyn said, coming into the gym to dress for volleyball practice. Our season started after football season and Coach had us practicing every day after school.

"Who?"

"Wyatt." She slammed open her locker next to mine.

"I thought you loved him."

"I'm mad at him."

"For what?"

"He wants to hang with his friends Friday night instead of going out with me."

That didn't seem like a "hate-able" offense to me. "You can't go out Saturday night instead?"

"He has to work."

I sat down to tie my sneakers. "You two go out all the time. Maybe he needs some guy time."

"So you're on his side?"

"Stop it. You're my friend."

She pouted. "I don't like being blown off."

"Tell me about it." My comment, meant to express how she often made me feel, went over her head.

Coach's whistle blew, signaling that we were all expected on the court.

"Go on," Elowyn said, looking dejected.

"I'll hate Wyatt too," I said, turning backward and moving toward the door. This wasn't hard since he'd never made any effort to even talk to me.

I never got the chance to hate him, though, because they'd made up by suppertime. The trouble was, problems kept surfacing. If Wyatt broke a date, they'd stop speaking for two days. If Elowyn shunned him in the halls, he'd sit with his buds during lunch instead of her. She'd ignore his calls and texts. I couldn't keep track of who was mad at whom and why. Then one December day, Wyatt came up to me while I was fiddling with my hall locker. He slammed the palm of his hand so hard against the metal locker beside mine that I jumped a foot. "What?" I screeched. "Are you trying to give me a heart attack?"

"Elowyn is psycho!"

"Don't talk about my friend like that." *She* was usually the one who beat a path to me with a list of gripes about *him*. I hesitated, then asked, "Now what?"

"I walked Jan Frickie to class and El saw us and had a meltdown. I mean it was nothing. We're in the same class and we were just walking."

"The blowup—public or private?"

"Private."

"That's good."

"She won't even speak to me. Ignores my texts and calls."

I sighed. "Anything going on with you and Jan?"

"No way! El's the one. She's crazy jealous. Sometimes I feel like she's swallowing me whole."

He looked so dejected, I felt kind of sorry for him. "Any ideas how I can fix this?" he asked. "She's really wacked-out and you can help. Please?"

The bell rang and I knew I was going to be late.

Inspiration hit me. "Text her in French," I said, tossing books into my locker and shutting the door.

"Are you kidding?"

"Try it. Make it romantic," I said, jogging away.

My advice worked, and before I knew it, I became the most-to-be-pitied of human life-forms: the go-between.

Elowyn turned sixteen on December twentieth. She got her license the same day, and her dad gave her the keys to her own car. "Birthday and Christmas," he told her. She was jumping up and down and screaming; I was staring, awestruck. I wouldn't be sixteen until March and I was certain there was no car in my future. I'd have to share Mom's old Honda.

Elowyn dangled the keys in front of me. "Let's go!"

Her car was bright red, with all kinds of bells and whistles. We hopped inside. The new-car smell was intoxicating and I breathed in deeply.

"Not too far," Terri called out from the front door.

"We still have cake to eat, Sugar Plum!" her dad yelled.

"Save me a piece!" Elowyn cried as she backed out of the driveway and spun the wheel.

"You be back in twenty minutes!" Terri shouted. "And fasten your seat belts!"

"Twenty minutes. As if!" Elowyn said to me. "Try the radio."

I found our favorite station. "Where are we going?"

"To show it to Wyatt. Where do you think?"

Not where I'd wanted to go, but I understood. I'd helped to negotiate another truce between them a few days before. Of course she'd want to show him her new car.

"I'll have a key made for you," she said.

Her words floored me. "To your car? I'm not legal yet."

"You will be. And until then, I'll be picking you up for school every day."

My mom usually drove us to school and Terri picked us up after practice. "That'll be so cool. Thank you!"

She grinned. "This will be our best year ever."

Unless you and Wyatt kill me with your squabbling, I thought, but I didn't say it. Elowyn had offered me the keys to her car, and I was happy to have such a wonderful and generous best friend.

· 3 ·

Kassey

Mom and I were in the kitchen when she said, "Your father wants to reestablish contact with you."

She dropped this bombshell on me right after New Year's.

"What? Why?" I was startled by the news. We hadn't heard from my dad in many years, and I hardly remembered him, since he'd bailed when I was three.

"According to this, he's turning his life around." She waved several pieces of paper at me. "He's catching up on back child support too. You may be able to go to any college you want after all."

I'd asked Mom questions about him when I was younger: "Why did he leave?" "Where is he?" "Why doesn't he come visit?" Then when I turned twelve,

Mom sat me down and told me the hard truth. My father was an addict, a druggie. She said, "I knew he had drug problems when we married, but I thought he'd give it up once he had a family. He didn't. When you were three, I told him, 'Us or the drugs.' He picked the drugs and I left with you and he disappeared." The story was unvarnished, unlaced with comforting words like "he loved you." Nothing but plain hard facts. She wasn't mean or angry when she told me, just factual. Her eyes held mine and her voice was steady.

The shock of the truth about my father turned me hot, then cold all over. I had started to cry. What ever happened to "just say no"? In my imagination, I'd made up a father who was an adventurer, a world traveler who trotted around the globe and who Mom had divorced because he was always gone. But from the moment since she'd told me the truth, I'd flushed him out of my heart. There was only Mom and me. I'd sprung from her body like a mushroom.

Learning my father was a drug addict repulsed me. At school only kids on the fringe messed with drugs. Alcohol and cigs were common, but not hard drugs. What hurt most was hearing that he'd abandoned us, throwing us away like an old pair of shoes. I felt so ashamed that I'd never told a soul about him, not even Elowyn. Now I was almost sixteen and he wanted contact. "Ha! What's he want from me?" I asked Mom.

"He just wants to get reacquainted. Well, acquainted. He's trying to make amends. You can e-mail him. He gave his e-address."

"Where is he?"

"Colorado."

"What should I do?"

"Whatever you want. This has to be your decision, Kassey."

My mom watched over me and always had. We were a team, mother and daughter braving the world together. I had no place for my father in my life or in my heart. "I don't want to contact him," I said. "Why should I? Just because *he* wants to?"

She looked at me for a long time, then finally she said, "Maybe someday you will."

I was pretty sure I wouldn't. I didn't even think about whether Mom would stay in touch or what she would tell him. I didn't care.

Volleyball season was in full swing by the end of January. Elowyn and I had moved up to the varsity squad and the local paper called us "the dynamic duo." Coach Collins called us "the Force." We were on a winning streak and I loved it. My grades were tops, my volleyball skills smoking, my friendships solid. Maybe Elowyn's statement that this would be our best year ever would come to pass.

I was at Elowyn's house, the news about my father wanting contact burning a hole in me. I wasn't used to keeping secrets from her. "So how are you doing in Wyatt-land?" I asked.

"Good, for now." Elowyn smiled, toyed with the locket Wyatt had given her for her birthday and Christmas and that she never removed.

"Good to hear," I said.

"Just wait until your birthday," she said with a grin, and held up the huge jangling key chain with the words *Friends Forever* set with sparkly crystals I'd gotten her for Christmas. "You can't lose this one in your purse," I'd said at the time.

She'd also given me a cashmere sweater plus slipped me a key to her car, which I'd stashed in a zippered compartment of my purse. "Six weeks," I said. "But who's counting?"

We laughed like crazy. Mom was to get off work early and I would take my driver's license test the day I turned sixteen. I couldn't wait.

On Wednesday night a week before Valentine's Day, I was holed up in my room with a geometry book, a furious thunderstorm raging outside, and flickering electricity. "Don't go down," I pleaded with the fluctuating current. Elowyn had wanted me to hit the mall with her after school, but I'd begged off. I had a huge test on Monday and this stuff was hard.

Rain slammed against the windows of my bedroom. Lightning flashed. I cringed.

My cell went off with the music I'd downloaded to signal a call from Elowyn. I grabbed it. "You find any bargains without me?" I asked cheerfully.

"It's over," she said, crying.

"What's over?"

"Me and Wyatt."

I slumped. "What happened?"

"I caught him with Jan Frickie. I was coming out of Macy's, the door nearest the theater, and he and Jan were standing out front talking and . . . and holding hands."

My stomach dropped. "Oh no. El, I'm sorry."

She cried harder.

I said, "Maybe there's an explanation—"

"Oh sure! They had an explanation all right. They'd just 'bumped into each other.' That's what they told me."

My heart thudded. "You talked to them? While they were together?"

"You bet I did! I hammered them both right there on the sidewalk, in front of everyone. I let them have it. Called him every name I could think of."

A public blowup; the gossip mill would be churning tomorrow. If anyone had seen them and had a cell handy, the whole mess might be posted on YouTube or Facebook within hours. Not good.

A clap of thunder made me jump. "Where are you?"

"Just driving around. Some old country road."

"It's pouring here."

"Here too."

"Go home. Call me later."

"I hate him . . ." Her voice trailed off. We lost the connection.

I paced the room, working up words to console her. *You're right, he's a creep. Jan went after him. He adores you, El. You!* Deep down I was thinking, *If I get my hands on you, Wyatt Nolan, you're a dead man.* No wonder I didn't want a boyfriend. Boys were trouble! They lied and cheated. The more I paced the madder I got. Wyatt was a snake.

At some point I sat down and picked up my geometry book. Studying for a test was over. I cleared my bed. Fuming, I stretched out, deciding that when Elowyn called I wasn't going to say a thing to encourage her relationship with Wyatt. I was tired of being the messenger and the fixer. It was time I told El to lose him—not because I was jealous, but because I hated to see her so upset. She could easily find another boyfriend. A line of guys was waiting to grab her up.

I woke from my cell vibrating against my cheek. I

had set it not to ring because Mom didn't allow me to take calls after ten and I was expecting Elowyn to get back to me. Disoriented, I sat up and looked at the clock bleary-eyed. Twelve-twenty. I snatched up the phone, flipped it open. "El?"

"Terri," the voice said. "It's Terri."

I sat up straighter. "Yes?"

With a tight voice, she asked, "Is Elowyn over there with you? She hasn't come home."

· 4 ·

Kassey

"Is she there, Kassey?" Terri asked again.

"N-no," I stuttered.

"Because if she is, if something's happened—just tell me the truth. I won't be mad. Her dad and I are worried sick."

"She isn't here, Terri. I swear. Cross my heart."

"Oh, God," Terri mumbled. "Have you heard from her tonight?"

"Yes! I did. She called me about eight." I wasn't sure how far to go with details.

"Where was she?"

"Driving home. On some country road."

"But why? Why would she be out in the country?"

"Um—to clear her head." My voice sounded

shaky and I realized this wasn't the time to hold back anything. "She—um—she'd had a fight with Wyatt."

"Was he with her?"

"No. She was alone."

Silence. She finally said, "I know it's late, but I'm calling his house."

"Terri," I blurted before she could ring off. "Please call me when you know something. Please."

Her voice softened. "I will, honey. My first call will be to you."

I was sitting at the kitchen table drinking coffee when Mom came downstairs at six-forty the next morning. She was partially dressed for work, having to leave the house by seven to get to her downtown office by eight in heavy Atlanta traffic. "What's this? I usually have to drag you out of bed." She looked hard at me. "Are you crying?"

I nodded.

She dropped down beside me. "What's wrong?"

"Elowyn never came home last night." Haltingly I told her what I knew.

"Her parents must be frantic," she said.

"Where could she be?"

Mom smoothed my hair. "Maybe she's at home by now and Terri's just waiting for a decent hour to call."

I shook my head. "She wouldn't do that to me."

Mom settled into a chair, took my hands in hers. "It'll be all right, baby."

I didn't believe her. Clutching at her hands, I said, "Mom, please don't make me go to school today." Without Elowyn to pick me up, I'd have to ride the bus, and it was due two streets over in fifteen minutes. "I—I can't sit in school . . . not knowing . . . anything. . . ."

"Tell you what," she said. "I'll call Kathy and tell her I won't be coming in until after lunch."

"You'll stay with me?"

"You shouldn't be alone while you wait to find out what's happened to your best friend."

I threw my arms around her and sobbed.

For once I was glad about the cell phone ban at school. I knew the news about Elowyn, about her public blowup with Wyatt, would be all over the building, and since I was her best friend people would be looking to me for details. I only wanted to talk to Terri. Mom and I sat by our phones willing them to ring. When my cell finally rang it was about ten o'clock. I almost jumped out of my skin. I grabbed it and said, "Yes?"

"The police found her in her car this morning," Terri said dully.

I screamed and Mom stood up and took the phone. She talked quietly, then hung up and said, "They've taken her to Emory Medical, neuro ICU. Get in the car."

The drive to the sprawling medical complex seemed endless and the February day—gray, cloudy, and cold—matched my mood. I didn't trust myself to talk, but Mom told me what Terri had said, which wasn't much. "Her car skidded off the road in the rain and hit a ditch. The air bag deployed, but she hit at an angle and didn't get much protection. A man walking his dog in a field saw the back end of the car sticking up from a ditch. It was lucky he came by because the car couldn't be seen from the road." Mom glanced over at me huddled in the corner of her car. "She's hurt bad, Kassey."

I squeezed my eyes shut. I wanted to cover my ears too.

"That's why she's at Emory. They're the best for head injuries."

Neuro ICU was a giant, dimly lit room behind a glass wall. Machines sat beside every bed and nurses worked as quietly as ghosts, checking IVs and monitors attached to silent, sleeping patients. The central nurses' station directed us to a family waiting room where we found Terri, her hands covering her face. When Mom spoke, Terri bolted from her chair and hugged her, then me. She smelled like coffee, mints, and fear. I started to cry but made myself stop. Terri didn't need me to fall apart. "H-how is she? Is she in that room?" I pointed at the glass room down the hall.

"In bed number eight. They only let us in for ten minutes every hour. She's in a bad way," Terri said, her voice husky.

Just then, Matt, Elowyn's dad, walked in with two cups of coffee. He looked haggard and grim. His skin had a grayish color. "Hey, Kassey . . . Susan. Would you like some coffee? I don't mind going down for it. Better than the stuff up here." He nodded toward a small table with a coffeepot and Styrofoam cups. The stink of burned coffee hung in the air and made my stomach queasy. I hadn't eaten anything this morning. Mom and I declined his offer.

"What else do you know?" Mom asked.

"In the accident her head was slammed sideways into the glass."

"My fault," Matt mumbled. "I shouldn't have bought her the car."

Terri took his hand, shushed him. "Don't say that, honey. It was an accident."

I remembered how happy Elowyn was with her beautiful new red car.

"Thank God she was wearing her seat belt or she could have been thrown from the car and killed," Terri said.

I thought back to the times we'd not worn our belts while driving. I wouldn't do that ever again.

"She has a massive head trauma and a broken foot—the foot probably from applying the brakes," Matt said. "Some internal bruising from the seat belt, but no other broken bones."

"That's good, isn't it?" I asked, hope growing in me.

"Bones heal," Terri said. "She has a deep brain injury with massive swelling. She's in a coma. Not so easy to come out of that."

My hope tumbled. "Can they help her?"

"They're trying to get the swelling down. It's not so simple."

It didn't seem possible that life could get so topsy-turvy in such a short amount of time. Only yesterday Elowyn and I had been at school laughing in the halls and feeling invincible after volleyball practice, talking about crushing Decatur in Friday night's match. Only yesterday she'd asked me to go with her to the mall. If I'd gone, she might not have been driving on that stretch of road. I'd have been with her and would have been talking to her, trying to defuse the situation with Wyatt. I should have been with her.

I asked, "Can I see her?"

Terri glanced at my mom. "I'd rather you not go in there today. Maybe tomorrow."

I was torn between wanting to see her and touch

her and the fear of doing either thing. Mom put her arm around me. "We'll come back later."

"But I don't want to leave."

Terri took my hand. A fine mist of tears clouded her eyes. "Please. Later."

We drove home in silence. My mom was always smart about knowing when to talk to me and when not to. I was grateful for that because my emotions were raw and ragged and I didn't feel like talking. As we rounded the corner of our street, I saw someone sitting on our front-porch step.

"I wonder who that is," Mom said.

As she turned into the driveway, I recognized the person wearing a gray parka huddled in the cold. I unsnapped my seat belt and flew out of the car even before Mom had fully stopped. I ran swinging my arms and snarling straight at Wyatt Nolan.

· 5 ·

Kassey

I pummeled him with my fists, flailing my arms and yelling the whole time. He didn't try to move away, just hunched over and covered his head with his arms. He didn't say a word, just kept taking my blows. I'm pretty strong from playing volleyball, so I know I was hurting him.

From behind me, I heard Mom shouting. "Kassey! What's the matter with you? Stop that! Now!" She tugged at my arms until she broke through my fury. She crouched next to Wyatt. "Are you all right?"

"Mom, don't—"

She whipped around and said, "You stop it! Stand back. I mean it. You don't go around attacking people. You're not an animal."

Wyatt looked up. "It's okay, Mrs. Mesacheck. I deserve it." His voice was flat. He was bleeding above his left eye. My anger deflated at the sight of his bright red blood trickling down his temple.

"Come inside," Mom said. "Let me clean you up."

I didn't want the traitor inside our house.

Mom gritted her teeth at me. "I'll deal with you later."

Much later, after Wyatt was patched up and we were sitting in our kitchen drinking colas, Mom said, "Tell me what set you off, Kassey."

"He cheated on Elowyn," I growled.

"It wasn't what it looked like," Wyatt said.

"What was it then?"

"I was meeting Jon Lewis at the movies, you know, to see that new action flick, the kind of movie Elowyn hates. I was waiting outside for him and he called and said his dad had grounded him and he couldn't come. So I was thinking about seeing it by myself when Jan sees me and comes over and we start talking. Turns out she wanted to see that movie too and she was by herself, so we just bought our tickets and went inside and saw it."

Jan was a snake. And hers was a crime of opportunity. I'll *bet* she'd come to see that movie.

Wyatt continued. "I didn't buy her ticket or anything. She bought the drinks and popcorn. All we did was sit together."

"And share popcorn," I said sarcastically. "How tender."

"Kassey," Mom warned.

"When we went outside after the movie, well, that's when El saw us."

"You were holding hands," I reminded him.

"Jan just grabbed my hand to say thank you."

I rolled my eyes. How can guys be so dumb!

"I wasn't cheating!" he cried.

"Do you know what's happened to Elowyn?" Mom asked.

He nodded. "Elowyn had a car wreck and she's in the hospital. It's all over school."

"How? I didn't tell anyone," I said.

"Her dad called in to the front office. Principal Banks announced it over the PA this afternoon."

"It was bound to come out," Mom said.

"Why did you come here?" I asked, emotion clogging my throat.

"Because you're her best friend. I figured you'd know more than anyone how she's doing. I want to know."

"Her family is at the hospital." I saw pain and fear and regret in his dark brown eyes. "Are you sorry because of what happened to Elowyn, or because you got caught with Jan?"

"Not fair," he said as Mom shot me another warning look.

I crossed my arms, slouched in my chair. "She's at Emory, in the neuro unit. That's how she is. She's in a coma."

I skipped school the next day too. Mom dropped me off at Emory and said she'd be back when she got off work, insisting that this was the last day I could skip classes. I hurried up to the ICU, found Terri in the family waiting area. She looked as if she hadn't slept a wink. "How is she?"

"No change."

My heart plunged. "I—I thought maybe . . ."

Terri shook her head. "We talked to her neurologist this morning. They keep doing a test on her . . . the Glasgow. It measures sensitivity to pain in a head-injured patient. A normal reading is fifteen. Elowyn's a three."

The news took the wind out of me.

"Matt's a basket case. I made him go home and clean up. I'll go when he comes back, then we sit and wait." She stared at me. "I'm glad you're here, Kassey."

"Does this mean I can see her today?"

"Actually, her neurologist wants the people closest to her to talk to her. He says that even when patients are in a coma, they don't lose their sense of hearing. If we all talk to her, maybe she'll hear us and . . ." Her voice broke. "And she'll come back to us."

"I can talk to her. I have a million stories," I said. Over the years Elowyn and I had shared our lives and had a lot of adventures. Surely she'd remember them and wake up smiling.

I turned toward the unit. Terri caught my arm. "She looks pretty grim. Bruised and swollen. Not like the girl you know."

Terri hadn't lied. Elowyn's head, swollen and wrapped in white bandages, looked huge, her face puffy. She looked like a giant marshmallow. I stored the word image so I could tease her with it when she was well. Her eyes were ringed with raccoon-like circles of red-purple, and her eyelids didn't quite close. IVs and tubes ran from every opening in her body over and under the sheets covering her. Her chest rose and fell with the help of a machine.

"A ventilator," Terri whispered. "Until she can breathe on her own."

The sight of Elowyn hooked to all that technology was shocking, like a blast of icy water on my skin. I shuddered. Elowyn's hand contracted and I jumped.

"Involuntary muscle reaction," Terri said. "I called a nurse the first time I saw it. It means nothing."

Tears filled my eyes.

"Just talk quietly. You'll have between ten and fifteen minutes alone."

She pulled over a chair and I sat close to the bed. Terri left and I leaned into Elowyn's ear. "Hey, girl-friend. It's me. . . ." I wiped my eyes, decided to start again. "Remember when we first met? Hospital. Broken bones. You wore pink pj's with little puppy paw prints."

Only the hiss of the ventilator answered me.

I reminded her of school, of summers at the pool.

The beep of her heartbeat on a monitor sounded robotic.

"Wyatt's sorry. Really sorry. He . . . he said it wasn't what it looked like. Him and Jan."

The hum of the hospital room's AC filled the quiet. Elowyn didn't move.

"Not that I forgive him. That's up to you. So you have to wake up and deal with him."

Nurses shuffled past, their soft-soled shoes giving an occasional squeak on the well-scrubbed floor.

"I slapped him around. Can you believe it? I really let him have it. He bled."

Beneath her hooded eyelids, Elowyn's pupils looked large, taking up all the space where her irises should be seen.

My voice trickled away. The machines were keeping her body alive, but where was she? Where was Elowyn?

· 6 ·

Kassey

The next day at school, people rushed me. They asked a hundred questions I couldn't answer, or didn't want to answer. I saw Wyatt in the halls, still wearing the Band-Aid Mom had stuck on him. We didn't speak. Jan was a pariah. Everyone shunned her, and I heard later that she cried in a girls' bathroom and went home early.

When Coach caught up with me, she asked questions too. "She's bad off," I told her, the words sticking in my throat.

"We still have a game Friday night," Coach said.

I'd forgotten about facing Decatur. "Coach, I don't think I can play."

"The team needs you. I can't lose my two best players at the same time."

I wanted to scream, *My best friend's in a coma! I can't think about volleyball!* Instead I said, "I—I just don't think I can keep my head in the game."

"Is that what she'd want you to do? Bail on the team? The girls are shook up, and you're the captain."

That was unfair. Of course Elowyn wouldn't want me to bail. I could almost hear her saying, "Don't be a wuss. Suit up. Kick Decatur butts."

Coach said, "If she wakes up between now and then, you're free to hang with her. But if she doesn't, I expect you to show up."

It sounded cruel and hard-hearted, yet I knew I had to play. I had to play because Elowyn couldn't. Because she might not play for the rest of the season.

Decatur stomped us. Coach begged, prodded, and pleaded with the squad, but our team fire was out. Especially mine. I kept playing the ball to Elowyn's spot on the rotation, but she wasn't there. She wasn't there.

After the game Wyatt came up and asked me if I wanted a ride to the hospital. Mom had given me permission to stay past my usual curfew if I wanted to go see Elowyn. I understood Wyatt's need to come—he just wanted to be close by, same as me.

We didn't have much to say to each other during the drive, which suited me just fine.

Terri hugged us both when we stepped into the waiting room. She looked ready to drop; still, she was gracious. "It's good to see you, Wyatt."

He didn't meet her eyes, and he looked as if he might cry. "I'm really sorry," he said.

"We all are. Do you want to see her?"

Terri's question surprised me because I didn't think Wyatt deserved to see her.

"Yes." Wyatt's voice sounded hoarse.

"Maybe you can reach her. We can't."

Terri's words made me feel as if I'd failed her and Matt and Elowyn. I reminded myself that Elowyn loved Wyatt. Love was supposed to be strong medicine. I told Wyatt, "You should talk to her."

He followed Terri into the unit, and they came out about ten minutes later. Wyatt's face was the color of chalk. He didn't say a word. He walked down the corridor and punched the button for the elevator. It wasn't until after he was gone that I realized my ride home was also gone. It was almost midnight and I'd have to call Mom to come pick me up.

Terri took my hand. "I'll take you home. Matt wants me to sleep at the house tonight. He'll return and stay with his Sugar Plum."

When Matt stepped into the room, Terri fell into

· 40 ·

his arms. I watched them hold each other for the longest time, and wondered what it would be like to have someone to lean on like they leaned on one another. I wondered if Mom ever missed my dad, then pushed the thought away. Why should she miss him? She'd given him a choice, and he'd chosen to leave us.

In the car, Terri was uncharacteristically silent. The heater turned me buttery warm, and within minutes I was falling asleep. The strain of the past few days, the exertion of tonight's game, the sadness inside my soul made me want to sleep for a year.

In my driveway, Terri turned off the engine and touched my shoulder, rousing me out of my stupor. "They want to turn off the machines," she said quietly.

"What?" I was suddenly wide awake. "But why?"

"Her doctors tell us she's fallen farther down on her test scores. They say she has an irrevocable deep-brain trauma and for all intents and purposes, she's experiencing brain death. Fixed and dilated pupils . . . doll's eyes, they call it. No response to pain. No upper-brain activity on her CT scans. The only thing keeping her alive is the machines. She'll never recover." Terri stared out the windshield, recited the facts and statistics in a voice without inflection.

"Never?" I couldn't process what she was telling me. Never was forever.

"Her body will begin to shut down with or without the machines."

"Do you believe them?"

She turned her face toward me. "My little girl's never coming home."

The car was turning cold and I shivered as I tried to wrap my mind around Terri's words.

She took a deep breath. "Did you know she'd checked the little box on the back of her driver's license to be an organ donor?"

"I—I don't think so." I dragged out the words in an effort to remember something. "There was a man who came to our school. He wanted to impress on us about safe driving. You know, not drinking and driving. And he told us that his brother was killed by a drunk driver, but that he'd donated his brother's organs to help others, so that his brother hadn't died for nothing. He told us that organ donation was . . . like . . . you know, noble. Elowyn and I talked about it. I didn't know she'd checked the box."

"Well, she did. The transplant people talked to us yesterday. They said her organs would go to help a lot of people."

"You're going to give her organs away?" The idea made me feel sick. Not organ donation in principle— the man's speech had been inspiring—but giving away Elowyn's organs. How could they?

"It's what she wanted done. She'll look perfectly

fine after . . . afterward. She'll look the same on the outside of her body. Her organs will save many lives and . . ." She didn't finish the sentence.

I almost gagged on my tears, but I didn't break down in front of Terri. "You're sure? About . . . her brain?"

She nodded, sniffed hard. "We're going to spend tomorrow with her. In a private room. If she's still unresponsive at the end of the day, we'll let them turn off the machines. A transplant team will be there. . . ." She broke down and couldn't continue.

Neither could I. I grabbed at the door handle, numb and blind with tears.

Before I could tumble out into the cold, Terri called, "Please come and say goodbye to her tomorrow."

I made it inside the house before I sank to my knees sobbing. Mom was waiting up and she ran to me.

"What's wrong, baby? What's wrong?"

I managed to tell her the story in spurts. She listened, found me a tissue, made me stand up and walk into my room. She sat me on the bed and slipped off my shoes, laid me down, and covered me with my comforter, the one Elowyn and I had bought together after we painted my walls purple and my furniture white.

I cried into the soft material. At some point, Mom crawled into the bed with me and held me, whispering soothing words in my ear. She comforted me as if I were a small child afraid of the dark, until my body stopped shaking and I drifted into a dreamless black sleep.

· 7 ·

Kassey

I was like a dead girl walking. Mom and I were on the surgical floor at the hospital, heading toward the private room where Elowyn lay still and hooked to machines. She was being kept alive to keep her organs usable. I knew that behind the huge double doors at the end of the hall a transplant team was waiting.

After talking to Mom for most of the morning, I was resigned to what was happening. I understood that parts of Elowyn's body would go to save others. I knew that with my head. But my heart had a hard time accepting the reality.

"Is that the way you'd want to live?" Mom had asked me. "Hooked to machines?"

"Would you turn me off?" I asked her.

"What would you want me to do?"

I saw nothing but brick walls. "I guess I'd want to donate," I answered. "It seems best. If I'm dead."

She brushed my cheek. "Like the Wicked Witch of the West in the *Wizard of Oz*? Really, most sincerely dead?"

I gave her a weak smile.

Terri and Matt were in the room with Elowyn, on either side of her bed, each of them holding one of her hands and weeping. The vent tube was taped to her face and the machine hissed softly, doing the job she could no longer do on her own. "Come in," Terri said. Her eyes were swollen and red. "Tell her goodbye."

Mom and I came closer. I stared at Elowyn's face. Some of the swelling had gone down and the skin around her eyes was turning from red to purple. "She looks asleep," I said. I wanted to touch her while her skin was warm and alive.

"Go ahead," Terri said, as if reading my mind.

I stroked Elowyn's cheek, hoping she'd flinch, wishing she'd sit up and say, "Cut that out!"

My throat filled with a million things to say, but my voice couldn't make its way out. I took a step back. Terri pulled me into her arms, held on so tight I could hardly breathe. I felt her trembling. "You were like a sister to her," she whispered in my ear.

I was blinded by tears.

"It's time to go." Mom put her arm around my waist and helped me to the open door. We made our way back down the hall, leaving Elowyn's parents alone with their daughter and her machines and the waiting transplant team.

Her name was Elowyn Eden.

She was my best friend.

She died when she was sixteen years old.

part two

· 8 ·

Arabeth

The call came early on a Sunday. I heard the phone ringing from upstairs, where I lay in my room in bed sucking oxygen from a big green tank parked beside me, my companion almost twenty-four hours a day. I heard Mom pounding up the stairs and then she threw open my bedroom door. Breathlessly, she said, "They have a heart."

I bolted upright. My heart fluttered from the exertion and the adrenaline rush.

Mom hurried to my closet, opened the door, and took out a suitcase, packed for months waiting for this call to come. "Don't move. I'll toss this in the car and then help you downstairs."

After dropping off the suitcase, she returned, helped me to stand, and switched my oxygen to a portable unit I could carry in my hand. I took a long look around my room, wondering when I'd see it again. Or if. In the car I said, "I hope this isn't another false alarm."

When I was thirteen, the call had come from Emory Hospital saying that the national donor service had a heart for me. The heart was being flown to Atlanta from another city in Georgia, and the transplant team was ready and waiting. We got to the hospital fast. I was prepped for the operating room, excited, ready for a new heart, a real life. I could run again! Jump. Go to a regular school. Then the big letdown when the heart had been declared unsuitable and I'd had to go home with my same old-same old.

"You're at the top of the list," my doctor had said, trying to console me.

I knew the transplant was based first on need, on blood and cell compatibility, and on body size—they couldn't put a giant's heart into a small kid. Being at the top of the list didn't matter if the other things didn't match. "What a way to be number one," I said. "No effort on my part. Just luck."

Now, a year later, here I was again, all hopeful, longing for the transplant to happen, for it to be over with, for me to finally be well.

Mom blew through a red light. "What if a cop stops our Batmobile?" I asked.

"Then he can give us an escort," she answered.

At the hospital nurses were waiting for me with a wheelchair. They got me upstairs, put me on a gurney, and began to prep me. A hospital gown, a paper cap on my head, IVs in my arms, electrodes on my chest. Dr. Chastain appeared in the room. "How are we doing, Arabeth?"

He's a cardiologist and head of the transplant team. In the OR, there would be an army of people to assist him. "Is it a good heart?" I asked.

"It is."

"Not like last time?"

"This heart came from a teenage girl, like you. She died from a head trauma."

Not like me, I thought. She'd been normal. "What else?"

He shrugged. Secrets are kept in the donor program. They won't tell you much about a donor, claiming privileged information.

"You remember what I've told you about the operation?" he said, changing the subject.

"Yes." How could I forget the gory details? I would be cut open like a fish, from my collarbone to my midsection. The transplant team would attach me to a heart-lung machine, cool my blood to protect my body and my brain, remove my old failing heart, and put in the new one. I would be clinically dead until the new heart was sewn in and restarted.

"A six-hour cakewalk," Dr. Chastain joked. "Got

to get all those little vessels reattached. I'm pretty good with a needle and thread, if I do say so myself."

"Maybe you can make a prom dress for me someday," I joked. I was getting sleepy from the drugs in my IV.

Mom took my hand. "Stay strong."

"Who do you suppose she was?" I asked. "The girl. I wish I could meet her family . . . tell them thank you."

"We're all grateful," Mom said. She leaned over and kissed and hugged me, blinking back tears. "I'll be waiting, baby. Me and Aunt Vivian and Uncle Theo. We love you. *I* love you."

"I love you too, Mom."

They wheeled me down the hall. I watched the overhead lights roll past. I'd been wrapped in warm blankets, but my hands were numb and my lips cold. This was it. No dress rehearsal. I thought again about the girl who'd died and her parents donating her heart to me, a stranger. Who was she?

Machines and people filled the OR. My brain felt fuzzy. Dr. Chastain bent over me. "Ready to sleep, Arabeth?"

I couldn't form words, so I nodded.

The anesthesiologist slipped a mask over my nose and mouth. The room blurred. My last thought was for my daddy. If only he could be with Mom while she waited.

. . .

An elephant was standing on my chest.

"Wake up, Arabeth," a voice kept saying. "It's all over. You have a new heart."

I struggled to obey the voice and open my eyes. The pain was horrible, the weight on my chest almost unbearable. I forced my eyes open, saw a nurse, and next to her, Mom.

"Hi, baby." Mom stroked my cheek. "You made it through just fine."

I had a tube down my throat. I couldn't speak.

"Look," she said. She carefully lifted my hand toward my line of vision. My nail beds were bright pink, not blue as they had been for years. Tears welled up. The new heart was pumping my blood to my fingertips, to every cell of my body. I was alive.

I'd been told that making it through the first twenty-four hours was a good sign for a good recovery. I flew through the first twenty-four hours and the next and the next. I felt so good, I sat on the side of my bed on day two, took a short walk with a nurse's help later the same day. I could breathe freely. I had energy. I asked, "Is this what it feels like to be healthy?"

Mom laughed. "Oh, honey, you look wonderful!"

"Your skin's pink as a baby's butt," Aunt Viv said.

I'd been put into a clean room, and anyone coming in to see me had to wear a mask and a sterile gown. Germs were my mortal enemy, at least until my drug regime stabilized my immune system. Of course there was always a chance of rejection, a possibility that my body would rebel and refuse to accept the new organ, so along with antibiotics, I was pumped full of anti-rejection drugs. "You'll have to take them all your life," Dr. Chastain told me.

"And puff up like a toad," I said. The drugs would show up in my face, filling it out until I looked like a moon pie.

"The effects will wear off," he said. "And they'll keep you from rejecting."

I would do anything to protect my new heart, even look grotesque.

Aunt Viv said she and Mom were going to give my bedroom at home a makeover. "What do you want?" she asked. "Any special colors? Style?"

My head filled with images of the colors yellow and deep blue and fields of pretty purple lavender plants waving in the breeze. "Yellow and blue and lavender," I said before I knew it. "You know, like in France."

"France?" Mom puckered her brow. "Where did that come from? It'll be different from the rest of the house. Are you sure?"

Mom owned a bed-and-breakfast in historic

Roswell, a suburb of Atlanta, where we lived. Our house was decorated in a rustic style with antiques and painted furniture, pine hardwood floors, and slouchy flowered sofas and chairs. We had four guest rooms upstairs, a large dining room for our guests, and a kitchen where Mom created Southern-style meals—not just breakfast, but lunch and dinner too. Our patio was surrounded by gardens. Mom and I lived in a newly constructed section at the back of the house consisting of two bedrooms upstairs and a small private family room on the main floor. She'd carried the country look through the whole house.

I thought about it. "I'm sure. I mean, as long you asked me to pick a style."

Mom and Aunt Viv looked at each other. Mom said, "Well, if that's what my girl wants, she shall have it. France it is."

Even I was puzzled by my choice. If any part of the world interested me, it was England—a place I'd read so much about in the works of Jane Austen. And yet, the impression of France was so strong in my mind, I couldn't have said anything else. Crazy.

I went home on a sunny April day wearing a mask for my own protection and with strict orders to remain out of public places for six weeks. "No shopping," Dr. Chastain told me. I had a long list of instructions and a plastic container filled with prescription pills. At the house Mom wrote appointments for follow-up visits in red on a giant wall calendar.

I felt good, and didn't want to be housebound. But I didn't want to get sick either.

When I opened the door to my bedroom, I could hardly believe my eyes. My bedroom had been transformed.

"Do you like it?" Mom asked.

"It's French country. We copied the colors and style from a decorating book," Aunt Viv explained.

"It's beautiful!" I said. The walls were yellow, the furniture pale blue and white. A pattern of sunflowers covered the bedspread and pillow shams. There were blue accent pillows with yellow trim, a framed poster of a water garden over the bed, and a bright red lamp on a new bedside table. The scent of lavender filled the air.

"So did we nail it?" Aunt Viv asked.

The skin on my arms and the back of my neck prickled. Something about the room felt familiar, but how could it? I knew nothing about France. I'd never so much as written a research report on the country. I'd never seen French country decor in my life, yet I felt at home in the bedroom. "It's perfect," I said. "Totally perfect."

· 9 ·

Arabeth

I've divided my life into two parts: the awful years and the truly awful years. I was an army brat, so we moved a lot. Mom was always packing and unpacking—new faces, new schools, new house. When I was six my heart started going down the tubes. It was a genetic thing and nothing that I couldn't live with at first. I played hard, stopped when I got winded. Simple. But that was the start of my awful years.

By the time I was ten, my heart was working way too hard and I had to slow down, stay inside in the summer heat, take naps like a two-year-old. Dad was promoted to sergeant and stationed in Texas, where I was close to a great kids' hospital and a doctor who watched over me. I heard my doctor use the word *transplant* a couple of times, and it made Mom cry and Dad look sad. That bothered me because I didn't want them to be unhappy.

Dad called me his princess and built me a playhouse in the backyard that was big enough for two to have tea parties and pretend to be real princesses. It was painted lime green with cheery pink trim, had a door that opened and closed, two windows and a table and three chairs inside. Every kid on the base living in army housing wanted to be my friend. Especially Monica. She came every day, and we shared everything in our heart of hearts with each other. In the playhouse we could be anyone we wanted. She wanted to be a movie star. I wanted to be a gymnast. The house was magic.

The truly awful years began when I was almost twelve and Dad got shipped off to Afghanistan for a two-year tour of duty. Then it was just me and Mom waiting for his letters, e-mails, phone calls. He sent me gifts: a few dolls—"This is what the local girls play with," he said—a beautiful kite, and for Christmas that year a camel saddle. I didn't have a camel to ride, so Mom put a hobbyhorse in my room and I threw the saddle on it. Weird-looking, but I loved it because it was from my daddy.

I started sixth grade with him still half a world away. My heart was getting weaker, but I dragged myself to school because being at home all day was just too lonely. Mom worked half days in the commissary and volunteered to help new army wives adjust to the army way of life. My social life wobbled. It was hard for me to keep up, hard to go places like the skating rink and the bowling alley. I was tired all the time and short of breath. I hung on to Monica, my only friend, but one day she came up to me in the hall and said, "I don't want to be your friend anymore."

I couldn't believe it. "Why?"

"I have new friends," she said.

Behind her, I saw a group of the popular girls, the ones who controlled the social order at the school. They were pretty, and catty, and Monica and I used to poke fun at them behind their backs. Now she was telling me she was one of them. I almost burst into tears. "But you're my best friend," I said.

"Things change," she said with a peek over her shoulder to see the others watching her.

Her initiation, I thought. This was what she had to do to join them—humiliate me and walk off into the sunset. It worked. I felt horrible. My heart squeezed and not from its internal flaws.

Stupidly I said, "But my playhouse . . ."

She smirked. "That's baby stuff. You play in your *dollhouse.* I'm doing other things."

She walked back to the group and they swished off down the hall. I went to the principal's office and asked to go home. I wasn't feeling good, I told the assistant principal. She called my mother and when I got in the car, the floodgates opened. I told Mom everything. "That's so mean," Mom said. "Do you want me to call Monica's mother?"

Horrified, I said, "No! Never!" I was twelve. I had my pride.

Pride was cold comfort when I sat alone in the cafeteria, or watched Monica and her new friends walk in a group down the halls. Worst of all, I never figured out why those girls blackballed me. Or why Monica went along with them.

Just before school ended that year, Monica's dad was transferred. For Monica, being transferred meant starting over on another base, in another state, in another school; it meant starting at the bottom of a new social order and making new friends. Maybe she'd pick nicer ones next time. I saw her crying alone on a bus bench on the last day of school, her little group of girlfriends nowhere around. I tried to feel sorry for her, but I couldn't. She never called to tell me good-bye. I shut myself in my playhouse and cried.

My heart was getting worse, and I settled in for the long hot Texas summer. I was already dreading starting seventh grade and going back to school, but I was also relieved because I wouldn't have to see Monica, the traitor, every day.

The day of the Great Awful came one late afternoon in July. I was sitting on our sofa writing a letter to Dad. He told both me and Mom that he liked letters best. Letters made him feel closer to us than e-mails, even though letters took longer to get to him. He also liked the care packages we sent—boxes of things he couldn't get in Afghanistan, like peanut butter, sports magazines, good soap, and especially Mom's chocolate chip cookies.

I saw the jeep pull up through the window and I sat straighter. The base commander and his aide headed for our door. The brass on the commander's hat glinted in the sunlight. My heart skipped beats. "Mom!" I yelled. She was in the kitchen starting dinner.

She came out quickly, wiping her hands on a towel. "What's wrong?"

"Commander's here."

We both froze. The doorbell rang.

Bad news from the army is delivered in person. "Go away," I whispered.

They didn't. They came in and told me and Mom that my daddy, Sergeant Gordon H. Thompson, had been killed by a roadside bomb on the streets of Kabul in Afghanistan.

I remember crying more than I've ever cried before or since. I remember other army wives coming over and bringing food and holding Mom while she cried. I remember going to Dad's funeral: soldiers in dress uniforms, the crack of rifles, a casket draped with an American flag, the perfect precision folding of the flag and the commander presenting it to Mom.

On the walk back to the car that would take us home, I fainted. I woke in Mom's arms. She held me on the grass, squeezing me and whispering, "Don't you die on me, Arabeth. Don't you dare!"

We packed and left the army base, went to Atlanta to Aunt Vivian's. We lived with her and Uncle Theo and my three cousins for a few months. Cindy, my seven-year-old cousin, was put out of her room so I could take it over until Mom figured out what we were going to do. "I don't like you," Cindy told me.

"No problem," I told her. "Nobody likes me."

With the money from the army, and her savings and Dad's pension, Mom bought the bed-and-breakfast in Roswell. I went into the homebound program for school. When the first heart transplant fell through, I withdrew into a really dark place inside myself. I turned fourteen facing the facts of my life. I had no dad, no friends, a malfunctioning heart, no future, and no hope.

And then one morning, the phone rang and I was offered a stranger's heart.

· 10 ·

Kassey

If funerals were supposed to bring closure, Elowyn's funeral didn't work for me. I cried nonstop for days, until Mom forced me to see a grief counselor. The woman told me nothing I didn't already know—the car wreck had been a senseless accident, it was okay to grieve but I couldn't let it control me, life went on . . . blah-blah-blah. She even suggested that I take an antidepressant "for a few months." I didn't want pills. I didn't want a counselor. I wanted my friend back.

I wasn't exactly shining on the volleyball court either. I still liked the game, but my teammates got on my nerves. None of them could play like Elowyn, anticipating my moves like she could read my mind. Coach called me into her office just before the playoffs. "Lighten up, Kassey. Don't be so aggressive. The girls are complaining."

"Well, they should work harder." *Whiners,* I thought.

"We made the playoffs. I'm proud of our team. It doesn't help morale when the captain is always shouting and criticizing every mistake. We can win this whole thing if we work together."

"Aren't you the one who used to tell us that mistakes don't win games?"

Coach blew air through her lips. "I know you're hurting, but you can't take it out on the others."

I had a zinger comeback but I bit my tongue because Coach won't tolerate back talk. "Yes, all right. I'll watch it."

We won the first game and the team wanted to go out for ice cream, but I didn't feel like celebrating. I looked up in the gym stands for Mom, who comes to all my games. As the bleachers cleared and kids streamed past me calling out "Good game," I caught sight of her in the top row, her back to the wall. Terri was sitting next to her. My heart stumbled. I hadn't seen her since the funeral and didn't expect to see her at this game.

Mom waved, and I watched her and Terri thread their way down the rows toward me. "Nice game," Mom said, giving me a hug.

"Terrific," Terri said.

"Thanks." I couldn't meet Terri's eyes.

She reached out and took my hand. "I—I couldn't stay away. I know how much Ellie loved volleyball and how hard she played the game."

"It's not the same . . . without . . ." I didn't finish because a lump had swelled my throat shut.

"We miss her too," Terri said. "More than I can say. Matt wanted to come tonight, but he couldn't face it."

Mom intervened. "Maybe we can go for coffee."

"I shouldn't intrude . . ."

"No," I said. "That's a good idea."

We went to Java the Hut, a coffee shop not far from the school. I got a syrupy fruit drink and Mom and Terri drank coffee. Elowyn and I never liked the taste of coffee much.

"I miss the activity too," Terri said, stirring her coffee. "You know, all you kids hanging around the house. It's so quiet now."

"I miss your cookies," I said.

She smiled, the corner of her mouth quivering. "I've put together two scrapbooks. Of our vacations and Ellie's school stuff. I have lots of time."

She sounded so sad. Mom reached over and took her hand. "We should go to the movies. Dinner too."

Terri nodded. I hung my head. "Kassey, you should come over and talk sometime. I'll show you the books."

"I will," I said. "I'd like to see them."

We grew quiet. Coffee cups clinked in the background. The espresso machine hissed, and someone's cell went off. Terri stared out the window next to our table as if she were looking into a black hole. I shivered. She said, "I haven't touched a thing in her room. I just shut the door and left it the way she had. Whenever I look inside, it's like she's coming back to clean up the mess."

"It was an organized mess," I said. "She knew exactly where everything was no matter how messy her room."

Mom cleared her throat. "We should be going."

"Oh, of course. Kassey must be tired."

"I'm fine," I said, without much conviction.

We stood. "I'm serious about you coming over for a visit," Terri said. "I'd love to see you." She hugged me and Mom and I watched her walk out the door.

For my sixteenth birthday, Mom gave me her Honda. I'd passed my driver's test in it the day before, on my actual birthday. "For me? But what are you going to drive to work?"

"A newer used car. We'll pick it up this afternoon." She grinned and hugged me. "It's stodgy. Besides, this old car is reliable and dependable. New tires, oil, maintenance up to date. I've paid the insurance and filled up the tank too. You'll have to supply all future gas."

I grabbed the key. "I'll get a job."

"In the summer," Mom said. "Right now, your job is school."

"And volleyball." I tossed the key high, batted it, and caught it before it hit the floor. "I'm going for a drive."

"Before Saturday pancakes?"

"Who's hungry?" I grabbed my wallet and ran out the door.

"Be careful," she yelled, looking anxious. The memory of Elowyn's accident was still fresh in both our minds.

"I will," I called, backing out of the driveway carefully. At the end of the street, I pushed the gas pedal and the tires squealed just a little as I picked up speed.

This was the best present in the world. I had freedom. Taking some babysitting jobs would keep me running until summer came. I got to the stoplight, turned right. Freedom. So what was I going to do with it? I slowed. The one person in the world I wanted to hang with was gone. My heart sank. I drove aimlessly. Minutes later, without even knowing how I got there, I realized I was on Elowyn's street and in front of her house. I stopped the car across the street, let the motor run, and stared at the brick house where she had lived. Maybe I should go in and say hello. Hadn't Terri wanted me to come over? But I couldn't make myself walk to the front door.

A persistent banging noise broke through my fog of indecision. I craned my neck and could just see over the big bush that partially hid the side driveway leading to the garage. That was where the sound was coming from. I backed up the car for a better view. What I saw chilled my blood. In the driveway was what was left of Elowyn's car. The front grill was mangled, all smashed and bent from its encounter with a tree. The glass was gone from the windshield and the fender on one side was missing. Matt stood on the car's roof, a sledgehammer in his hands. He swung it over and over, striking the crushed red metal, as if punishing the steel for not doing its job of saving his daughter. With every swing, I heard him grunt and curse. I watched, mesmerized, wishing the car could scream with pain because it had let us all down. Without even seeing his face, I knew that he was crying. This father wanted his daughter. I pushed thoughts of my own father out of my head. Did he even remember it was my birthday? I could only think of El and the love her father felt for her.

I watched until the sound of the hammer bruised my ears, until Matt could hardly lift the heavy iron tool. With tears running down my face, I slid the Honda into drive and slowly inched away, the joy of my birthday sliding down into despair.

· 11 ·

Arabeth

My new heart was becoming part of me. In three months, the side effects of my meds began to subside and my face looked more normal. The doctor had laid out my regime—antirejection medications for the rest of my life; eight, perhaps ten biopsies during the first year to detect the possibility of rejection; blood work every two months. I hated the idea of being a medical guinea pig, of going to the hospital for seemingly endless labs, but it was what I had to do.

"Things will change," he told me and Mom. "Once you make it past the first year safely, you'll come in for an echocardiogram twice a year and an annual angiogram. Blood work will be an ongoing event, but you're young and this is a strong heart.

Never take a medication without medical approval, okay? You could trigger a rejection episode."

Of course, I understood and I agreed, but I sure didn't have to like it.

I was getting stronger every day and was able to help Mom at our bed-and-breakfast. Summer is our busiest time and our guest rooms are usually booked solid, especially on weekends. I helped her change linens, vacuum, clean bathrooms, cook big breakfasts—all the things she'd had to do by herself while my heart was collapsing.

She was anxious at first. "Are you sure you're not overdoing it, honey?"

"I feel great," I told her. And I did. Who ever thought dusting and vacuuming could be liberating? But it was for me.

One afternoon when I was helping Mom change bedsheets, I said, "I wish I knew more about my donor."

"You know as much as I know—she was sixteen and in a car accident."

"I wish I could tell her family thank you."

"Me too," Mom said, tucking in a corner of the top sheet. "It couldn't have been easy agreeing to donate your child's organs to strangers."

"Would you do it? I mean, if I were healthy and my organs were in good condition?"

"I wouldn't have thought so at one time."

"But now?"

"I've seen firsthand how it's changed our lives. I see my girl all glowing and taking deep breaths and jogging up stairs and being normal. It's changed the way I think about all of life."

I smoothed the quilt Mom threw on the bed as she talked. "I wish Daddy could see me now."

"Me too," Mom said. "He'd be so happy."

I felt the sharp edge of loss. I thought it had dulled over the years, but I was wrong. It seemed as if my new heart was just as capable of breaking as my sick old one had been.

"But I want to go to Roswell High."

"Out of the question," Mom said over the dinner table a month before school was to start.

I felt as if the wind had been knocked out of me. I'd been planning my classes and my wardrobe for days, excited to be going to the big public high school. But now Mom was telling me that I had to attend a small private school not far from where we lived. I'd been thinking about the kids I would meet, the boys I'd flirt with, and now my plans were going up in smoke. "You know that's not what I want. I've been looking forward all summer—"

"It's what I want," Mom said firmly. "You were

fortunate to even get into the Athena Academy. If your grades hadn't been so good—"

"Then remind me to turn stupid! I'm not going there." I shoved my chair back from the table. How would I ever get a boyfriend if I was trapped with a bunch of girls all day long?

"Sit down," Mom ordered.

Years of a structured military upbringing kicked in and I sat.

Mom leaned forward. "I want you safe. I want you in a smaller school so that if anything happens—"

"Nothing's going to happen. I'm fine. My doctor said so."

"You're doing well, but you're not completely over your transplant. It's too soon for you to throw yourself into the fray of the real world."

"No way!" I yelled.

She grabbed my hand. "Stop it! What's gotten into you, Arabeth? This isn't like you to argue and fight. But just so you know, I'm not changing my mind. You're going to Athena and that's that."

I crossed my arms defiantly.

Her face softened. "I promise you, if you have a good year, if you do well physically, I'll let you go to Roswell next year if you still want to."

My lips trembled from anger and disappointment. I didn't want to spend my sophomore year in classes with a bunch of girls. But I knew my mother. Once she made up her mind, the topic was closed. I choked down a few more bites of supper before leaving the table and going to my room.

I paced the floor of my bedroom, fuming. Catching sight of myself in the mirror, I stopped cold. The girl in the glass hardly looked like me. I turned to stare at my reflection. Why had I gotten so angry? Weeks before, I'd been terrified of attending Roswell— and of boys. I had never even had a real conversation with a guy my age; I didn't know any. And now I was fighting with my mother about a world that existed only inside my imagination.

Maybe it was the thought of all those girls, strangers, catty girls who might wreck my life with mean remarks and cold shoulders like Monica and her circle of friends had done. "Fifth grade is over," I reminded myself. Atlanta was a new city. I had a new heart. I was a new person. For another second, I wondered about the life of the sixteen-year-old girl whose heart beat inside me. I believed she'd never been a mean girl. I just knew it.

I had to go to the Academy—I called it AA, like the rehab places where alcoholics went—to take placement tests. "It's an entrance requirement," Mrs. Hawkins, the headmistress, told me the day I went. "Based on your transcripts, I'm sure you'll do just fine."

She walked with me, showing off the school and grounds. Mom had already done this when she chose the school so she decided to wait in Mrs. Hawkins's office. The school was stately and beautiful, with canopies of magnolia trees, red brick buildings, and modern, well-equipped classrooms. Although I tried to stay prejudiced against it, I couldn't.

Eventually Mrs. Hawkins took me into a room and laid out several packets of paper. She said, "These are standardized tests—fill in the circles for the right answers. The last page of number four is for a brief essay. We like to get an idea of your writing skills. It's just asking for your thoughts and plans for your future. You'll have an hour." She smiled and left the room.

My plans. Did I have any? I'd spent years just surviving. Now I had a future. What *did* I want?

The tests were easy. The essay, not so much. I was still writing furiously when Mrs. Hawkins came back into the room. Startled, I looked up.

"Time's up," she said, walking over.

I was still clutching the pencil midsentence. "I— I haven't finished."

"Not a problem. Your mother's told me about your health issues."

Her comment went right through me. "I don't need special treatment," I said defiantly.

"And you won't be getting any." She looked down at my paper, only half written. Her face broke into a smile. "You're a southpaw. So am I."

"A what?" I asked.

"You're left-handed."

I glanced at my hand holding the pencil, then dropped the pencil as if it had turned fiery hot. "No," I said. "I—I mean, I'm right-handed."

She looked puzzled. "But you're writing with your left hand."

I went cold all over, then warmth spread up my neck. "Um—not really."

"Then you're ambidextrous. Even better." She took the pencil, folded the tests, and reminded me my mother was waiting.

I stood up shakily and followed her out of the room. She was talking every step of the way, but I wasn't listening. All I could think about were the words on the paper I'd written, every one with a strange backward slant that wasn't exactly my handwriting.

· 12 ·

Kassey

Mom sent me to stay with my grandparents the summer before I became a junior. It was really hard to find a summer job so I was willing to go. "Better than moping around the house," she told me.

Not by much. I missed home. I missed Elowyn. As it turned out, my grandparents comforted me because Grandma taught me how to bake all kinds of pastries and Grandpa taught me how to use a table saw. Together we built a new deck in their backyard. They didn't ask me to talk about Elowyn, respecting my desire to keep my feelings to myself. Only once did Grandma mention something I didn't want to talk about, and it wasn't about Elowyn. We were rolling out dough for pie crusts one morning when she said, "Your mom told me that your father has begun making back support payments."

I stiffened. "Yes, she told me too."

"She says he wants to get reacquainted with you."

I shrugged. Sunlight streamed across the table, puddling on the flour and the cream-colored dough, turning them ghostly pale.

"You don't want to?"

"He left when I was really young. I barely remember him."

"Steve was a nice man. An engineering major. Got a good job right out of college too. Your mother was happy at first. But the drugs—well, they got a stranglehold on him and he couldn't break free."

"I don't do drugs, Grandma." I balled up the dough and restarted my roll-out.

"I never thought you did. This isn't about drugs, Kassey. It's about your father. He's the only one you'll ever have. He's reaching out finally."

"Mom could get married again," I said stubbornly.

"That's true. But Steve will always be your real father. Don't be so tough on him. He's trying to get his life back. . . . Consider giving him a chance to get to know you. It's never too late."

Irked, I pounded the dough ball to stretch it, and it split. I mashed the two pieces together with attitude. "I'm not interested in getting to know him. He left us.

I just lost my best friend. I've got a hard year of school ahead. I'm not ready for a hugfest with a father who left us."

The refrigerator hummed in the quiet room. Grandma rolled her circle of dough expertly until it was paper thin, tossed it gingerly from hand to hand, and spread it gently across a pie plate filled with fresh blueberries. Without looking at me, she said, "Be careful with that dough, honey. Handle it too rough and it turns tough as nails."

On the first day of school, I walked in the front doors, and my heart took a nosedive. In the "Noteworthy Student" glass case on the wall beside the front office was an eight-by-ten photo of Elowyn bordered in black. Below the picture were her obituary and a tribute written by one of the faculty. My vision went teary and I couldn't read it.

"Didn't expect this," a voice said next to me.

I turned to face Wyatt and for a second I lost my composure. "I miss her."

"Me too."

He'd grown taller, and looked tan and fit. "You still mad at me?" he asked.

I turned toward the glass case. "Guess not." I heaved a sigh. "Sorry I beat up on you. I was just really angry. I know what happened wasn't your fault."

"No problem." He gave me a sideways glance. "I've taken worse on the basketball court. Besides, you hit like a girl."

I snapped, "I drew blood." He grinned and I backpedaled. "Good thing for you I'm a girl. Otherwise I could have destroyed you."

"I carry the scars." He touched his forehead.

The tide of incoming students had thinned and except for a few stragglers, we were alone in the front vestibule. "It isn't fair," I said. "Her dying."

"Not one bit." His voice sounded thick.

The thread of Elowyn's memory held us together for a moment longer. We blinked in unison and the thread broke. We turned and hurried off down separate hallways and away from the smiling photo under the cold hard glass.

The memories turned out to be our glue. She linked us. Other kids remembered Elowyn, but Wyatt and I were the most affected by the loss of her. We sort of fell in with each other, at first just saying hi in the halls, then occasionally eating lunch together in the cafeteria. Then we began showing up at each other's games and going off afterward when the mood struck. We talked and texted and hung out. No big deal. We were like two spheres who intersected whenever we needed to exorcize Elowyn's ghost. It comforted me in a way that sessions with the grief counselor never had. The shared memories, the inside jokes between us, the stories we told about our times with her bound us together. We laughed and sometimes we cried, but the time I spent with Wyatt talking about Elowyn soothed me like cuddling with my baby blanket had when I was a little girl.

One night after Alpha had won a blowout volleyball game, I was freshly showered and dressing in the gym when Patti Aymon strolled over to me. "Wyatt's outside waiting," she said.

"I know. I'm hurrying."

She didn't go away.

"You need something?" I said.

She cocked her head. "You and him got a thing going?"

I whirled to face her. "What?"

"You and Wyatt. You're together a lot. People are talking."

"People should mind their own business."

She threw up her hands. "Hey, don't kill the messenger. It's just a question. I mean, everyone would get it. He's cute. He was your best friend's guy."

"So what's your point?"

"Nothing." She said it in a way that meant "something."

I gritted my teeth. "I don't like being talked about. And I don't like your insinuations. Wyatt and

I are friends. Just friends. We have someone in common that we both cared about. Neither of us is over her dying. Now take a hike and don't you ever gossip about me again. I don't want my best friend's boyfriend. I want my best friend."

I grabbed my jeans and sweater and finished dressing in a bathroom stall.

· 13 ·

Arabeth

There's an advantage to attending an all-girls school—there's no pressure to impress boys. There's also a disadvantage to attending an all-girls school—there are no guys to impress. The yin and yang principle. But there's a bigger negative too. Everybody already has their friendships and cliques cemented in concrete. I'm not the only new girl this year, but there aren't very many of us, so we stand out. During the second week of school, after gym class, someone noticed the top of the scar that runs from my breastbone to my navel.

"What happened to you?" asked the girl.

I clutched my shirt to my throat. "Surgery," I mumbled.

"What kind of surgery?"

I fiddled desperately with the numbers on my locker dial. *Let it go,* I begged silently. I didn't want it all over school that I'd had a heart transplant. "When I was younger," I said evasively. "No biggie, but it left a scar."

The girl was looking at me like I was a freaka-zoid. Which was just what I didn't want. My mind flashed back to standing in the hall with Monica telling me she had new friends, implying that these friends were more fun than sitting around a play-house with a sick girl like me. "Got to run," I told the nosey girl staring at me. I scurried off.

Later, when I told Mom about the incident she said, "Why not tell the truth—you had a heart trans-plant that saved your life."

She didn't get it. "I'll be an insect under glass. What if they talk about me?"

"Because you had a transplant? That's a stretch, Arabeth."

"They'll have a ton of questions I can't answer. Like who was your donor? How does it feel to have someone else's heart? Is it icky? I don't want to be some science experiment."

Mom looked shocked. "I thought you were grateful."

"I am. But talking to girls is different. I just don't want it spread around."

Mom sighed. "I don't see your problem."

You're not a fifteen-year-old girl wanting to blend in, I thought.

"I guess the only people who need to know are in the front office," Mom said. "And your teachers."

"And they already know and they're not supposed to talk about it," I said.

Before she left the room, Mom said, "You're different, Arabeth. Ever since the transplant, you've been different somehow, not like yourself. Not all the time, just sometimes. That's not a criticism," she added quickly. "Just an observation."

I'd felt it too, but I didn't dare confess it. I didn't dare tell her about the essay I'd written with my left hand or how I'd practiced ever since to do it again and couldn't. Of how holding a pen in my left hand felt awkward and weird and that any letters I managed to make looked like a four-year-old had drawn them. "Maybe I'm different because I'm older and for the first time in years, I feel good."

"Yes, you're growing up," Mom said, looking wistful.

And growing away, I thought, but didn't say.

"Maybe that's it," she said, without sounding persuaded.

We wear uniforms to Athena—navy or ivory golf-style shirts and khaki skirts or slacks. I was disappointed at first, but then I realized that the uniforms made all the girls equal—no over-the-top clothes, no designer labels and I'm-richer-than-you posturing. Sometimes wealth and privilege show up in the purses they carry, or in their computer bags—who knew Chanel made computer bags out of genuine crocodile hide?

Not all the girls at Athena were silver spoon queens. Some were on scholarships or were recipients of special grants. Maybe some were like me, beneficiaries of Social Security and military government funding. I thought about that sometimes—that my father dying in action a world away enabled me to attend such a prestigious school. I'd trade every bit of this education to have him back.

Athena was growing on me, but I never really felt as if I fit in, as if I belonged. I was definitely going to go for public school next year, no matter how much Mom tried to talk me out of it.

On the one-year anniversary of my transplant, Mom splurged and took the two of us out to dinner at a really fancy restaurant in downtown Atlanta. She ordered a glass of champagne and said, "To your good health," and let me take a sip.

"The bubbles tickle," I said.

She set the glass down and looked at me. She looked as if she had something to tell me.

"What?" I said.

"I've been in communication with your doctor about your heart."

My last labs were good. I wasn't due for more tests for a couple of months. "Is he recalling it?"

She laughed. "No, silly. He said he'd been contacted by the transplant center. He said that in rare occasions, if all parties are willing, they allow donor families and recipients to meet. They used to keep them apart, but research showed that often the two parties want to meet. That it was healthy for them to know one another. The donor family gets to see the value of donating their loved one's organs, and the recipient gets to express their gratitude.

"He said there are Web sites where recipients and donors search for each other. So the medical people sometimes facilitate the meeting. If everyone wants to. If—if the recipient is still alive. That's why they wait at least a year. It's an adjustment period."

Her words tumbled over me like a waterfall. When the flow stopped, I asked, "Are you saying that her family wants to meet me?"

"Only if you're willing."

I sat back in my chair, feeling like the wind had been knocked out of me. Hadn't I always wanted to tell them thank you? Hadn't I been wanting details about my donor? "Do you think I should?" I asked.

"It's your choice, Arabeth. In this case, I won't tell you what to do."

Great. She usually told me exactly what I should do. The heart in my chest picked up its pace. I had the chance to have so many questions answered. I had the chance to meet the family who had given me renewed life. How could I refuse?

"You can think about it. You don't have to make up your mind tonight," Mom said.

"I'd like to meet them," I blurted. "More than anything."

Misty-eyed, Mom reached over and clasped my hand. "I'll tell your doctor. He'll make the arrangements." She squeezed my hand. "I'm so proud of you, honey. And your dad would be too."

The heart in my chest settled down into a steady rhythm.

· 14 ·

Kassey

"Can you come over?" Terri asked me on my cell. "I have something for you."

I hadn't seen her since November when I'd run into her at the mall. Now it was January and almost a year since Elowyn's death. "Sure. When?" I was dreading going over to the house, but Terri had asked me to come over ages ago and I hadn't. I never told anyone about seeing Matt attacking El's wrecked car, but I knew I'd never forget that image.

"Tomorrow afternoon?"

Tomorrow was Saturday and I had no other plans. "After lunch?"

"See you then."

· · ·

I pulled up in front of the Edens' house, half expecting to see the rusty hulk of Elowyn's mangled car, but the side driveway looked clear. I got out of the car, walked to the front door, and rang the bell. Terri answered and hugged me instantly.

"You look wonderful," she said.

I stammered, "Th-thanks."

She looked thin, and tinier than I'd ever seen her. We stood at the front door and talked. She asked me a few general questions that I answered politely. Finally she said, "Do you want to see her room? How we've changed it?"

"No! "Um—sure," I said.

My heart was hammering hard when she opened the door to Elowyn's old bedroom. It had been totally transformed. Gone was any reminder that the room had once been a bedroom where Elowyn and I held countless sleepovers. The French decor had been replaced by cream-colored walls and built-in work surfaces, a sewing center, and floor-to-ceiling bookcases. Terri said, "This is my hobby room now— where I sew and do my scrapbooking. We kept the door shut for eight months, until Matt said it was time to change things. I didn't want to, but I couldn't come in here without falling apart. We thought about selling the house and moving, but I couldn't do that either."

I felt sorry for her. As much as I missed Elowyn,

I had school and volleyball and hanging out with friends to keep me busy. Terri and Matt had only memories. The look of Elowyn's room might have changed, but its purpose was still to honor her life.

The bookcases were heavy with scrapbooks. Terri followed my line of vision. "I take the books apart and reconfigure them all the time. I thought it would make me sad, but it doesn't. It comforts me to re-arrange the photos." Terri stroked the bindings of the upright books. "I have Christmas ones, her school days, vacation times. And just when I think I've fin-ished, I come up with another idea, so I tear books apart and build new ones."

A lump clogged my throat. I cleared it out. "You said you had something for me . . . ?"

Terri snapped out of her reverie. "Of course." She went to a large built-in desk strewn with ribbons and pieces of material and opened the top drawer. She re-moved a small box and handed it to me. "I found it when I was cleaning out her closet. She'd hidden it behind her sweaters."

I took the blue box tied with a white bow. "How do you know it's for me?"

"I peeked." Terri smiled. "I'm sure it was for your birthday last year."

I stared at the box. TIFFANY & CO. was written on the lid. Elowyn's favorite store. I remembered the times we'd gone in the store at Phipps Plaza and walked around gawking at the jewelry in gleaming glass cases. China was on the third floor and Elowyn had pointed out the crystal, china, and silver patterns she was going to request when she got married. "A little soon, don't you think?" I'd teased.

"Never too early to figure out what you like," she'd said.

"Maybe your tastes will change."

"Unlikely. This looks so European and fancy. I love it."

"What if your fiancé doesn't like it?"

She flashed a dreamy smile. "Like that will happen. He'll want me to be happy. And beautiful china will make me happy. We'll have parties and friends over and I'll light candles and our table will be gorgeous."

I understand why dishes and silverware meant so much to her. The china and silver and beautiful crystal helped her dream of happily ever after and of her future, things I hadn't thought too much about because Mom and I lived day to day with what we had—secondhand dishes and garage-sale finds. Terri had wonderful taste and Elowyn had inherited it from her mother. Both their dreams were gone now, vanished on a rainy road on a February night.

"Aren't you going to open it?" Terri's voice pulled me into the present.

I untied the ribbon and lifted the lid of the box.

Inside lay a silver bracelet with a single round disk. BFF was engraved on one side; my name was on the other. Tears blurred my sight.

"Let me help you put it on," Terri said. She draped the bracelet around my wrist and secured the clasp with trembling fingers. "It's beautiful," she said.

I sniffed. "I'll never take it off," I said. "Never."

Terri stroked my hair. Tears brimmed in her eyes. My heart felt like it was breaking in two. "I miss her so much," she said.

I held on to her and we cried together for a long time.

When I showed Wyatt the bracelet, he rolled the silver disk in his fingers and asked, "What do you want to do on the one-year anniversary?"

Of her death. He hadn't said the words, but we both knew what he meant. The anniversary of the day all our lives had changed was about a week away. I thought for a minute and said, "Something French."

The February day came, cool but clear. No rain. When school was out, we found a small art theater showing a French movie with subtitles. Midway through, Wyatt leaned over and said, "My head hurts trying to follow this. Can we split? She'd understand."

I didn't need encouragement.

Outside it was dark, though it was only seven o'clock. "Any ideas?" he asked.

"Food," I said. "French food."

"We can't afford some fancy French restaurant."

So we went to a specialty grocery store and cruised the aisles, picking up products and reading the ingredients on the backs of boxes and cans looking for food from Elowyn's favorite country. "Brie," I said, holding up a wedge of imported cheese. "All the way from France."

He sniffed it, shrugged. I put it into the cart.

"French bread," he said, tossing a baguette into our cart.

I thought it was cheating because the bread was baked in Atlanta, but I didn't argue. "Snails?" I picked up a long, skinny, see-through container stacked with snail shells.

We stared at the orderly pile of escargot, said "Eww" in unison, and put the package back on the shelf.

"Grapes," Wyatt said. "Aren't they French?"

"Sure . . . pressed into wine."

"Don't have my fake ID card with me," he said.

"Don't even go there," I told him, and pushed toward the bakery section.

"How about these éclairs for dessert?" He pointed to the cooler cases.

The chocolate-covered éclairs looked yummy. "Get two."

"I can eat more."

"Two," I told the woman behind the counter firmly.

In his car, I asked, "Where to?"

"I'll surprise you." He put the car into gear and drove on to I-85 and merged into the fast-moving traffic.

"You do have a plan, don't you?"

"I have a plan."

He got off thirty minutes later at the airport exit, found a few back access roads off the main drag, turned off his headlights, and drove along bumpy ground. He stopped along a deserted stretch of land in front of a high fence with razor wire at the top. Curiosity ate me up. "Is this legal?"

"Come on." He opened his door.

"Where?"

"Paris."

He pulled me out of the car along with the bag of food and an old blanket. He threw the blanket on the hood of the car, helped me up. The hood was still warm from the engine and the heat felt good through my clothes. He threw part of the blanket over our shoulders and started pulling food from the bag. He said, "Dig in."

We ate cheese and bread, grapes and grape juice,

and the éclairs. He toasted Elowyn and we touched our plastic cups together. Just then, a huge jet came rumbling along the asphalt on the far side of the fence. I clapped my hands over my ears and watched it gather speed, then lift screaming off the runway and soar over our heads. We were close enough to see its silver belly and retracting wheels. I crouched, feeling the rumble of its engines shake the ground.

"It won't hit us," he shouted above the roar.

I followed the plane with my eyes until I lost in the night sky. Goose bumps broke out on my skin. "Is it really going to Paris?" I asked.

"I'll bet so," he said.

I turned to him. "How do you know about this place?"

"We used to come here. El and me. She loved to hear the planes and watch them fly over us. She always said she'd go to Paris."

"The cops never stopped you from sitting here?"

"Never been caught. Besides, this runway is way far away from the actual airport. No one comes out here."

"Except for you and Elowyn."

"Not for a long time."

I poured us each some more grape juice and raised my glass to my friend, trying hard not to cry. "To Elowyn. We miss you."

I looked skyward, watching the blips of lights of

ascending and descending planes, mechanical fireflies filled with life, coming and going, high above the earth on the way to somewhere, someplace. Beside me, Wyatt put down his cup, turned my shoulders toward him. I stared into his dark eyes. Without warning, he cupped my face in his hands and he kissed me.

· 15 ·

Arabeth

"You're going to wear a hole in the floor," Mom said.

I paused, toyed with the strings of my hoodie, then went back to pacing. "When will they get here?"

"When they get here," she said. "Now sit down. I can't afford a new wood floor."

I plopped down on the couch, pulling the strings of my hoodie in a seesaw motion. "What if they don't like me? What if they're sorry they gave me their daughter's heart?"

"Now stop that," Mom chided. "They're going to like you and you're going to like them. So am I."

It had taken almost a month for the arrangements

to be made for us to meet my donor's parents. Mom and I had been surprised to learn that they lived so close by, just miles away in Alpharetta. I had imagined that my heart had been flown in dramatically via helicopter like I'd seen in TV shows, but that wasn't the case. We'd picked this Saturday in April to meet because the weatherman had predicted a glorious sunny day and I wanted the day to be perfect. Outside, tulips dotted our flower beds and dogwood and lilac bloomed. I smelled the lilac blossoms through the open window.

I heard the crunch of tires on our gravel driveway and shot off the sofa. My hands shook. "Do I look okay?"

"You're beautiful," Mom said.

I stole a peek out the window. A blue SUV was parked in front of the porch and a short, stocky man with dark hair was walking around to the passenger-side door. He opened it and took the hand of a tiny blond woman, helping her slide out of the vehicle. She held a purse and a tote bag. My heart thudded hard as the two of them walked up on the porch, these strangers and parents of my donor. The doorbell rang and I jumped. "Get it, Mom," I said.

Mom opened the screen door and the man and woman stepped inside. My heart was thumping like crazy. Mom introduced herself.

The man said, "Matt and Terri Eden."

The woman—Terri—stared at me. "And you?" she asked.

"Arabeth," I managed through wooden lips. My heart was beating so hard I thought it might fly out of my chest.

Terri stepped in front of me. Tears filled her eyes. "You have my daughter's heart." A statement, not a question.

"I do."

Suddenly Mom was at my side. "Why don't we all sit down." She guided me to the armchair across from the sofa. The Edens sat on the sofa. They couldn't take their eyes off me. I felt like a gawky kid, all elbows and knobby knees and sweaty palms—not one bit the poised teenager I wanted to be.

"Tea?" Mom said. "Cookies?"

She picked up her teapot handpainted with violets and a plate of homemade sugar cookies from the coffee table. Only Mom would think to serve food on such an extraordinary occasion.

Matt took a cookie, but didn't eat it.

"You're pretty," Terri said.

I blushed because she was being nice and trying so hard. "Thank you," I mumbled. "And I mean thank you for . . . for donating your daughter's heart to me."

"Random selection," Matt said, to remove them

from the process. "Donor services made the choice. Based on need."

"I needed it," I told him. "I was dying."

Mom poured tea for all of us. The sun caught the delicate bone china and shone through it, turning the cups creamy white. "We can never express our gratitude," she said. "Your daughter—tell me about her."

"Her name was Elowyn," Terri said.

"Pretty name," I said.

Encouraged, Terri pulled a large book from her tote bag. "This is a scrapbook I put together when I found out we were going to meet you. It's all about her life."

I took it, smoothed my hands over the cover. It looked handmade. I opened it and saw an eight-by-ten photo of a lovely blue-eyed blond girl. The dates of her birth and death were lettered in calligraphy below the picture. The date of her death coincided with my rebirth. A lump clogged my throat. Until now, the girl had no form or substance. Now I saw how real she had been. I thumbed through the book briefly, then closed it. "Could I keep it awhile? I want time to really look through it."

"Of course," Terri said. "Keep it as long as you like. Our address and phone number are on the inside back cover. You can call us to ask any questions you want."

"This is kind of you," Mom said. "I have pictures of Arabeth growing up, but I didn't think to pull them together. Silly of me. I know you might want to know about us."

"Yes," Terri said. "We would."

I was younger than Elowyn, and a whole lot less glamorous-looking. She would have been a junior in high school. She was probably popular and had a ton of friends, all of whom missed her horribly. I grew sadder by the minute.

I deferred to Mom to give the Edens a brief history of our lives. Terri's eyes widened when she heard about my father's death, but she never took her eyes off me while Mom talked. I felt squirmy and my heart never stopped thumping. The whole thing was harder than I'd thought it would be, this talking about the dead between us. My daddy had come home in a casket and we hadn't been allowed to see him—he was too messed up, we were told. The Edens at least got to see Elowyn's face before closing the lid of her casket.

I was so grateful for the gift they had given me—Elowyn's heart, strong and young. It sustained me, gave me life. I startled when I suddenly realized that Terri had asked me a question. "Yes?"

"I asked if you liked any sports? Have you ever played anything?"

"Not for a long time. I stopped running when I

was eight. I would get too out of breath because of my heart. Did Elowyn play?"

"Volleyball. She was good."

"I watched the Olympic beach volleyball games. The American team was awesome."

Terri's eyes filled with tears. Matt leaned over, took her hand. "We should go now, honey," he said. "Arabeth can call us after she's gone through your scrapbook."

He looked to me for confirmation. I nodded vigorously. "I will call," I said. "I know I'll want to know more."

They stood and so did Mom and I.

"You can call anytime," Mom said. "We're so grateful."

At the door, Terri turned to me. "May I touch you?"

I held out my hands and she grasped them like a lifeline. I wondered if she could feel my blood pulsing through my fingers, pumped by Elowyn's heart. I said, "Thanks for the book. I'll be real careful with it."

We went out onto the porch. On the top step, Matt turned and smiled at me. "You'll never know how much this means to us, meeting you."

"Good for me too, Sugar Plum."

The words fell out of my mouth so fast, I had no control over them. I clamped my hand over my lips, stepped back. Matt's face went white.

"What did you say?" he asked.

I kept my hand tight across my mouth and shook my head.

"Do you know why you said that? How did you know?"

"Know what?" Terri asked. She was still behind me at the door with Mom, but Matt's reaction made her hurry to his side. "What's wrong?"

I felt blindsided, like I'd cursed at them. "I—I'm sorry . . ."

"She said 'Sugar Plum' to me," Matt said.

Terri stared at me hard, her eyes wide and startled. "'Sugar Plum' was Matt's pet name for Elowyn."

"I—I didn't know," I stammered.

Mom put her arm around me. "I don't think Arabeth meant any harm."

"Right, right," Matt said. "It just shocked me. No harm done." His face looked pasty.

Terri slipped her hand into Matt's. "Maybe you saw it written in the scrapbook when you flipped through it."

I nodded, unable to explain my outburst.

"Sounds logical," Mom said. "Subconscious thing." She laughed nervously.

I agreed, although I was positive that wasn't what had happened. I told them goodbye without meeting Matt's eyes. I went back inside the house, grabbed the scrapbook, and hurried to my room. I needed to know a whole lot more about Elowyn Eden, the girl who sometimes seemed to be speaking through me, causing me to say and do things I'd never said or done before.

· 16 ·

Kassey

"So you're just going to continue to ignore him?"

"You said it was my choice, Mom." I was folding a basket full of clean laundry when Mom came into the living room and cornered me with her question.

"It is your choice. I just thought you might have softened toward him a little by now. He keeps sending me money and he always asks about you."

"In other words, as long as the money comes you think I owe him something."

That stopped her cold. I went back to rolling socks and folding T-shirts.

"I divorced him, Kassey, but he will always be your father. We both created you."

"And you stuck with me. He left."

"Payback? Is that what this is?"

No amount of arguing about it was going to change my mind about dear old Dad. I liked my life the way it was. I didn't want him in it. This year for my birthday, he'd sent me a check for a hundred dollars. I still hadn't cashed it because I felt like he was trying to buy a response from me. Besides, my mind was too full of other stuff to deal with the problem of my father right now.

"It isn't payback," I said. "I can't explain it. Please stop asking me about it."

"He just wants to communicate with you. That's all."

"You communicate with him. Why don't you marry him again—then we can all live together like one big happy family. Until I graduate next year, then I'm out of here if he moves in." I jerked the basket of laundry off the sofa where I'd been working.

"That's uncalled for. Don't sass me. I'm your mother."

The go-between, you mean, I thought. "I'll let you know if I change my mind."

I hurried to my room with the clothes and shut the door firmly behind me. I flopped down on my bed and chased my thoughts in circles. I wasn't thinking about my father, but about the thing that consumed all my waking thoughts—what had happened on the first anniversary of Elowyn's death. Why had Wyatt kissed me? He'd caught me off-guard, and shocked, I'd pushed him away, as if I'd been stung.

"Hey," he'd said, stroking my hair, looping a curl around his forefinger. "It wasn't supposed to hurt."

"It didn't hurt."

He lifted my chin and kissed me again slowly. Then he pulled me closer.

Caught in his arms, with the taste of him on my mouth and my insides on fire, I felt myself melting into a puddle, and wanting more. I surprised us both when I ducked my head, twisting my body to one side. "No," I said. Trembling, I slid off the hood of the car. "Can you please take me home now?"

"What's wrong?" He looked confused.

"I want to go." I wrapped my arms around myself, shivering with the cold.

"I don't get it. We were having a good time."

"Please," I said. " Just drive me home. We are only a 'we' because we are mourning Elowyn."

We hardly spoke during the long drive. He kept stealing sidelong glances at me, but I focused my attention straight ahead. In front of my house, I grabbed the door handle. He caught my arm. "We still friends?"

"Sure." I bolted for the front door.

The next day in school, he acted as if nothing had happened and nothing had changed. But for me a lot had changed. I felt guilty. He was Elowyn's boyfriend. It was as if she were standing in the dark behind me, her arms crossed, a look of disbelief on her face. *How could you, Kassey? I trusted you.*

Had I betrayed her? Friends don't go around letting another friend's guy kiss her. *She's gone . . . a whole year gone.* And yet I couldn't let go of the feeling that I'd done something unforgivable. Why? The honest truth was that I had liked it. Wyatt's lips had been soft and warm and the warmth had spread to the center of my body. It wasn't fair that the kiss I liked and that meant something to me should never have happened. It certainly never would have happened if my best friend hadn't died.

I was trying to sort out all these crazy emotions and feelings—figuring out why kissing Wyatt felt both good and bad and if this had anything to do with steering clear of my father, and wondering how my life fit together—when I got a call from Terri. "We met the girl who got Elowyn's heart. She lives in Roswell, can you believe it?" Terri said excitedly. "I loaned her a scrapbook and have talked to her twice since. She wants to know if—if she could meet you too. Would you be willing to meet her?"

· · ·

I had no one to share the news with except Wyatt. "Are you jerking me around?" he asked.

Taken aback, I said, "Why would I do that?"

"You've been mad at me for weeks. And now you're acting like we're best buds because El's mom calls you. What's your message to me here?"

Apparently he made no connection between kissing me and being Elowyn's boyfriend. No guilt at all for Wyatt Nolan. I felt my face get hot and returned to the main topic. "I'm telling you the truth . . . the girl who received Elowyn's heart lives in Roswell. And she wants to meet me. I figured you'd understand how weird this is to me."

He slumped back in his cafeteria chair. The sounds of dishes, of kids talking, of dropped silverware were all around us. An ordinary day. Except that it wasn't.

"You going to meet her?" he asked.

"Sure. Why wouldn't I?"

"Kind of creepy."

"Creepy? What do you mean? You know her organs went to other people to help someone else live. Somehow the heart seems different than the other organs, and the recipient is someone almost our own age. Here's a chance to meet this girl. I want to know all about her. I don't understand exactly why, but I feel compelled to, now that it's possible."

He scraped back his chair, stood, and picked up his tray. "It won't bring El back."

Nothing would bring Elowyn back.

The first Saturday in May I was to meet her at her house, a bed-and-breakfast. To say I was curious and yes, a little scared, put it mildly. The girl, this Arabeth Thompson, had Elowyn's heart inside her chest, keeping her alive. A miracle of medical science, but a transcendent experience for me. Maybe Wyatt was right—maybe it was creepy. But my desire to meet her and talk to her overrode my doubts, and I pulled up in front of her house on Saturday afternoon. A couple of cars were parked to one side of the old Victorian house and a sign proclaimed: WELCOME TO THE HONEYSUCKLE INN BED & BREAKFAST. DINNER SERVED DAILY.

Pots of violets surrounded the freshly painted white porch arranged with white wicker furniture. The screen door swung open and a long-legged girl in jeans with long dark hair stepped out. "Kassey?"

"Yes."

"I'm Arabeth. Come sit down." She gestured to a sofa with flowered cushions.

On a glass-topped table in front of the small sofa lay one of Terri's scrapbooks. I'd recognize it anywhere. My heart was pounding and my mouth was bone-dry. A part of Elowyn lived inside this girl. My eyes got misty.

"Tell you what," said Arabeth. "I'll get us some water. Oh, and how about some ice cream? Everything's better with ice cream."

I nodded, not sure I could keep my voice from quivering.

Arabeth grinned. "How about a dish of Chunky Monkey? It's my favorite."

· 17 ·

Kassey

Chunky Monkey. Elowyn's favorite flavor. By the time Arabeth returned with a tray holding two water glasses and two bowls of ice cream, I had regained some composure. She set the tray on the table next to the scrapbook and handed me my dish of ice cream. I stared into the cold mixture, realizing I hadn't eaten or even tasted the flavor for over a year. "How long has this been your favorite?" I asked.

"Not too long. I was always a plain vanilla girl, but one day I was in the grocery store passing the freezer cases and I looked over and saw the row of Chunky Monkey cartons inside. I just stopped in my tracks. I don't know why, but I just had the biggest urge to try it. So I bought it and it's been my favorite ever since."

I stirred the mixture with my spoon, took one small bite, and thought I might burst into tears. I set down the bowl on the table. "Brain freeze," I said.

"That happens to me a lot," Arabeth said. "I don't know why I crave the stuff. It's loaded with calories."

I poked the bowl with my big toe. "Elowyn liked it best too."

She looked up at me, startled. "Really?"

"I'm guessing it's a lot of people's favorite," I said dismissively.

Arabeth set aside her bowl, her expression thoughtful. She rocked in the small chair across from the sofa. She stared at me like she had something to say but wasn't sure how to say it. Finally she asked, "Can I tell you something?"

"So long as it isn't about aliens and flying saucers."

She stared hard, like I'd spoken in a foreign language. "Oh, you're joking."

"Not a very good joke," I said. "Tell me something."

"Ever since—" She stopped, started again. "I woke up from the transplant and ever since then many—some weird stuff has been happening to me."

This grabbed my interest. "What kind of stuff?"

Her face flushed. "You'll think I'm crazy."

I could tell she was troubled. "We're all a little crazy, I think."

A small smile lifted one corner of her mouth.

"Okay, here goes." She took a deep breath. "I like things I've never liked before. I think things I've never thought before. I do things I've never done before."

"Like . . . ?"

"The most recent? Wanting to meet you." She picked up the scrapbook. "When I looked through this, when I saw pictures of you and Elowyn together, I got this feeling of utter happiness. My heart went all fluttery and I wanted to laugh out loud. It was like I knew you and hadn't seen you in such a long time and you and I were—" Words failed her. "Close," she added lamely.

I got goose bumps, and a shivery feeling shot up my back. I'd never seen this Arabeth before in my life. I scooted into the sofa, away from her eager face.

"See? I told you it was weird."

"What else?" This girl was creeping me out. I wished Wyatt was with me.

"Like the ice cream just now. Why *that* flavor? There are a million flavors, but I hone in on the one that was her favorite."

My heart thumped hard and I felt as if I'd run a marathon. "Coincidence," I said without conviction.

"The worst was the day her parents came to meet me."

Terri hadn't said a thing about anything strange happening.

"What happened?"

"I—I said something. He was the only one who heard me. You know, Matt, her father."

"He loved her a lot."

"We were on the porch and he'd taken a step down and Terri and my mother were back near the door and I stepped up behind him and he was telling me how good it had been to meet me and I said . . ." Her eyes were wide and sincere. "I said, 'Good for me too, Sugar Plum.' That's what I said, and he went white as a sheet. Like he'd seen a ghost. And I have no idea why I said such a stupid thing to him."

By now my goose bumps had goose bumps. This was beyond weird. "It's what he used to call her."

Arabeth looked sad. "That's what they told me. I can't imagine where I came up with it."

I had nothing to say.

She said, "I don't know why these things are happening to me."

I sure as heck didn't know either, but I felt like spiders were crawling on my skin.

"I have some questions about the people in the scrapbook," Arabeth said, changing the subject. "I don't want to bother her parents. Can I ask you?"

I nodded. She picked up the book, opened it, flipped it toward me, and pointed. "Who's this?"

Wyatt grinned out of the picture, his arm slung casually around Elowyn's shoulders. I recalled the photograph because I had taken it. It had been after a volleyball game, at a time when they'd hadn't been crabby with one another. A grab shot that turned out like a million bucks. "He was her boyfriend."

"I guessed that. She was happy when this was taken. He didn't always make her happy, did he?" Arabeth smoothed her hand across the picture.

The movement looked intimate and her words surprised me. Shamed me too, because Wyatt and I had kissed. "Did you have a reaction to him too?" I asked, remembering what she'd told me about seeing my picture.

"I got happy and sad at the same time. I—I got a lump in my throat just looking at them together."

There was plenty I could have told her about Elowyn and Wyatt. Who'd known them better than me? Instead I stood up. "Look, I've got to be going."

"Really?" She looked disappointed. "I have more questions."

"I—I have an interview for a summer job." The interview wasn't for another week, but I wanted to go. My brain felt overloaded, like I was being bombarded by data I couldn't compute. How could this Arabeth have such an inside track to Elowyn?

"Can you come back?" Arabeth asked.

I wanted to yell "No way," but I heard myself saying "Sure."

Then I hurried to my car, anxious to put distance between me and the girl with Elowyn's heart. And, without explanation, the memories we shared.

Because there was no one else I could talk to, I flew to Wyatt's house. He was cutting the grass, and when I drove up he turned off the mower and jogged to my car. I said, "Got a minute?"

"You look like you've had a bad day."

"Thanks for the compliment."

"That's not what I meant. You just look wound up."

He opened my car door and I climbed out. We sat under a shady oak tree in his front yard, and I started talking about my meeting with Arabeth before we'd settled down. I told him everything, spilling my guts in rapid spurts, telling things out of order, backtracking, repeating myself, my tongue snapping over words like gunfire.

"You're spooked," he said.

"You got that right. She knows stuff. Who knows stuff about someone she's never met?"

"El's parents might have told her things."

"Like 'Sugar Plum'? Get real."

"Okay, it doesn't make sense." Wyatt pulled his knees to his chest and rested his chin on them. "I want to meet her."

"She didn't ask to meet you."

"Don't care. Be a friend and arrange it."

"Why?"

"I want to meet her for myself. Check out the things you've told me."

"Don't you believe me?"

He grabbed my hand and his eyes held mine. "I believe you. But if she says she has questions, who better to answer them than you and me?"

Linking us together like a couple didn't sit right, but I had no power to refuse him. "I'll talk to her," I said, and pulled my hand from his.

· 18 ·

Arabeth

I watched Kassey drive off, feeling as if I'd blown the visit. I should have kept my mouth shut. Stupid! Stupid me! Without a doubt she thought I was a nut job. Of course she wanted to know how I knew the things I did. So did I. I kicked the bowl of ice cream and sent it rolling across the porch floor, spilling a gooey mess in a stream. I swore I'd never eat Chunky Monkey again, no matter how much I craved it.

Mom took me shopping for summer clothes before school let out. I kept choosing items off the racks that caused expressions of disapproval from her, and when I couldn't ignore her anymore, I asked, "What's the problem?"

"Your tastes have changed."

"Is that bad?"

"No," she said too quickly. "Just a comment."

I pulled on a top with sparkles across the chest. "Maybe I'm sick of jeans and plain tees." I admired myself in the mirror, watching the sequins and small sparkles twinkle in the light. "I wear uniforms to school. I'm sick of dull and drab. Besides, everybody's wearing this stuff."

Mom picked up the price tag and blanched. "I'm not paying this for a T-shirt. The price is outrageous."

In truth, the shirt wasn't me at all, and that was problematic because I wanted it. I felt compelled to own it, to change something fundamental inside me. "I'll work extra at the inn all summer."

Mom eyed me. "Take it off. If you want something like this so much, then we'll go to the fabric store and buy a kit for you to redo some of your old shirts."

"Make one? Mom, no one does that."

She ignored me and stepped out of the dressing room. I knew the conversation was over. I fumed as I fumbled my way into my boring clothes.

Athena Academy had a ceremony to celebrate the graduating seniors and the passing of us other girls to the next grade level. I became a sophomore, but if I got my way, I'd be attending the big public high school in the fall. But on the night of the ceremony, the headmistress threw me a curve. I was offered a full scholarship because of my excellent grades, an honor given to just three underclasswomen in the school.

Mom was so thrilled, she almost popped a cork. At home, I kicked off my shoes, saying, "You promised me I could go to whatever school I wanted next year."

Her jaw dropped. "Are you saying you want to turn down this opportunity? Are you serious?"

My back was up. There would have been a time when I'd have fallen over this opportunity, but right now I felt like getting my way. "You *told* me I could choose."

Mom stared at me and I knew she was weighing her words. At last she said, "I can't even imagine why you'd trade a first-class education—a paid-for education—for a lesser education at a public school."

"That's not fair. Roswell High is a good school."

"Athena is a *great* school."

"It's not what I want." My body went hot. I knew she was right, but I couldn't let go of it. "I don't want to go to Athena in the fall."

"Think!" she demanded. "Athena is a free ticket. With a diploma from Athena, you'll be eligible for a first-class college and for good scholarships. You're smart. You've done so well. Don't walk away from this opportunity."

I felt like shouting "I'm a social reject, Mom!" How would attending Athena help me in the one area I wanted so much? I was boring and dull and friendless. And forget about me ever having a boyfriend. I was a girl with a stranger's heart inside me and a colorless future ahead of me.

"Look," she said, her voice soothing. "Let's just step back. I don't like fighting with you. You don't have to make a decision now. Let's see how the summer goes. You may feel totally different by the time school starts."

My head pounded. I was in a tug-of-war with forces I couldn't define and desires I couldn't grab hold of.

I'm smart enough to know that life is defined by seminal moments that are mostly unplanned and unexpected. A friend who dumps you in front of the coolest girls in school. A jeep stopping at your front door on a steamy hot afternoon. A phone that rings and a voice that says, "We have a heart." These moments became touchstones of my life. But the one that blindsided me that summer was the one that arrived with Kassey on a hot morning in June, a boy most amazing, who made my heart leap and my pulse race from the moment I first laid eyes on him.

Kassey had called the day before and asked, "Can I come over?"

I was astounded because I never thought I'd see her again. "Absolutely," I said.

She drove up in her car, an old Honda that looked like a freedom chariot to me. I was barely fifteen, with a learner's permit and a year to go before I could get my license. There was a passenger in her car and when I stepped out on the porch, I squinted to see who she'd brought with her.

When Wyatt stepped out of the car, he was his photograph come to life. My heart almost stopped, then leaped with a joy I couldn't contain. I wanted to run down the steps and hurl myself at him. I gripped the porch railing to keep me steady and to stop me from following through on my impulse.

"Hello," he said, looking up at me. "I'm Wyatt Nolan. I'll bet you're Arabeth."

"I'm Arabeth," I chirped like a parrot.

He bounded onto the porch. He was a force of nature with a hundred-watt smile. I stepped backward, unsure of what to say or do.

"Remember me?" Kassey asked.

My face burned for momentarily having forgotten she was coming up the steps with him. "You're Elowyn's friends," I said. "I'm glad you're here. There's so much I want to know about her."

"We knew her best of all," Wyatt said.

"Then maybe you can tell me about her. And why I feel like she's looking over my shoulder even though—" I stopped myself.

"Even though she's dead?" Wyatt offered, finishing my sentence. His expression had turned guarded.

I'll bet I turned five shades of red, each deeper than the one before. "I'm not making this up," I said.

Kassey stepped around Wyatt. "I don't think you are," she said. "We're here to help you figure it out."

· 19 ·

Kassey

I knew things were going to go weird from the minute Wyatt got out of the car and faced Arabeth. She was smiling at him with utter delight, as if he were a long-lost friend—an intimate friend, as if she knew what he looked like naked. It made my tummy twist. Sure, Wyatt was good-looking, but she'd only seen photos of him, so why was she looking at him as if she were ready to pounce? I shook my head to chase away the disturbing image.

"Sodas?" Arabeth asked, never taking her eyes off him.

"Sounds good," Wyatt said, looking dazed.

"All right," I said, not sure I could keep anything down.

When she went inside, I grabbed his arm. "What's going on? You look blown away. Do you know her?"

"Never saw her before in my life." He faced me. "It was a trip, though. She . . . she reminds me of—"

I interrupted. "Don't say it. She's not her."

"It was déjà vu," Wyatt said. "Like I was seeing through a time warp."

"Arabeth doesn't look anything like her. Not one bit."

"True. But it's not this girl's looks. It—it's something else. I can't explain it."

Neither could I, but the impression was definitely there—Arabeth *felt* familiar. Thinking back to our first meeting, I had been struck then by a sense of commonality with her. When she'd brought out the ice cream, I'd been unnerved. I had more questions for him, but just then Arabeth came out the screen door carrying sodas on a tray, the same tray she'd used for the bowls of ice cream.

"Grab one," she said, setting the tray on the wicker table and sitting in the rocking chair. That left the sofa for me and Wyatt. We sat awkwardly. She continued to stare at Wyatt and he at her. She said, "I know that technically we're all strangers, but when I sit here seeing you both . . . well, you don't seem like strangers to me. Does that make sense?"

It did, but I wasn't going to say as much.

Wyatt chirped in with "It does to me."

"Maybe it's because you've seen the scrapbook," I suggested, shooting Wyatt a "chill out" look. "Power of suggestion."

"I've pored over it," she confessed. "Sometimes a picture seems as if I've seen it somewhere before. It's like grabbing smoke, though. I can't ever quite catch it."

Her face was troubled. I had no choice but to believe her. "So what do you think is happening?" I asked.

The rocker squeaked on the painted wooden porch floor. The June heat felt like a damp blanket on my skin. She held my eyes with hers. "I wish I knew. Maybe I'm just going crazy."

"Then so am I," Wyatt said. "Because I feel like I know you, and I don't."

Their gazes connected and I felt heat pass between them. In one fell swoop, I felt myself shoved aside, like a forgotten and unimportant item in a stack of old clothes.

"Could you have been a little more fawning?" I snapped sarcastically at Wyatt as I drove us home.

"What?" He sounded irritated.

"You were the skeptic before you came today."

He shrugged. "I can't deny that something's going on here. Don't tell me you don't think so too."

I did, but I was cranky and feeling out of sorts. "So what are you going to do to figure it out?"

"Not sure."

I was sure. "You going to date her?"

He stared out the window, but I knew I'd hit on his thought line. "I'll see her again for sure."

"She's fifteen, Wyatt. You're seventeen."

"So?"

"She's a kid." I felt threatened and didn't understand why.

"I'm not going to marry her, Kassey. I just want to get to know her better. Don't you?"

She gave me the creeps. "She isn't Elowyn," I said.

"I know that." He picked at his thumbnail, a nervous habit of his I'd noticed over the past several months of togetherness. "But you got to admit that she reminds you of El. Crap, Kassey, she even smells like El. She must use the same perfume."

I'd noticed it too. "She's strange," I growled.

We didn't speak again until I dropped him off. "You mad at me?" I asked.

He leaned into the window. "I just can't figure you out. We both think this whole thing needs to be examined, but you act like I'm committing an act of treason when I say I'm going to get to know her better. What's with you anyway?"

I only wish I knew. "Call if you come up with any answers," I said, and drove away.

· · ·

At home, I opened my e-mail on Mom's computer and sorted through the messages, all mostly junk. One e-mail stopped me cold. It was from my dad. He'd left it to me to contact him and I never had. Now he was making first contact. What had happened to my message of "leave me alone"?

I started to push the Delete button, but realized I couldn't. Mom wouldn't understand and my guess was that he'd tell her. I opened the e-mail.

Kassey,

I would have liked this to have been a response to an e-mail from you, but I couldn't wait any longer. I had to write. I want to ask your forgiveness for leaving you and your mother years ago. I was wrong. Certainly I can blame the drugs and the hold they had on me. I can blame my own stupidity for walking away from the best thing I ever had going—my family. But to put the blame on anything except my shoulders is a cop-out. I'm an addict. It took me years to admit it, two years to clean up.

I'm clean now and working in Colorado and rebuilding my life. I have no illusions that I can have what I threw away with you and your mom, but I do want to have a relationship with you both. Susan has been in touch and has forgiven me. I'm grateful. That leaves only you. Susan has told me that you need time to accept me again, to believe I'm for "real." I accept that. I'm not rushing you, not begging you. I only want you to know I'm sincere from the bottom of my heart. You're my only child. I've missed years with you. I want to know you. My heart is always open, my life recommitted to being a father to you.

Contact me anytime. I love you.
Dad

Well, there it was, my dad longing for togetherness. My dad asking for forgiveness. My mom had already forgiven him! Didn't they realize I'd been hurt and robbed? It's not so easy to say "Sure, all is forgiven." I struggled against a knot of emotion rising in my throat. My feelings were raw nerve endings. I'd been so long without a father in my life, I didn't know what I felt anymore. I didn't know how to accept him or where to fit him in. I had so few memories of him. No birthdays, no Christmases, no holidays of any kind. He was a blank wall in my mind. Maybe even an intrusion.

As I tried to conjure up memories of my father, all I got were images of Elowyn's dad, Matt. He was my standard-bearer for fathers. She was his Sugar Plum. When we were younger, he'd tell us both, "You two are the prettiest trout in the pond. I'm going to have to beat the boys off with my fishing pole."

Elowyn would twirl and say, "Oh, Daddy, I'm prettier than an old fish. And don't you go threatening the boys with sticks either."

Matt would tip his head. "Not much prettier than a trout leaping out of the water on a fall day."

"Daddy!"

Then he'd hug her hard and pat my head. "You know I'm joking, honey. There's nothing better-looking on this earth than my baby girl." And he'd add for my benefit, "Or her best friend."

Matt was a shining example of fatherhood to me, my own dad, a shadowy flicker.

I left the e-mail in my inbox. I didn't answer it, but I didn't delete it either.

· 20 ·

Arabeth

I've never had a boy's undivided attention until Wyatt came along, and it about blew me away. The first time he called me, my heart felt like it was going to hammer itself into smithereens. He called on our business line, and I answered, "Honeysuckle Bed and Breakfast. How may I help you?"

"Arabeth? It's Wyatt. How're you doing?"

My voice stuck in my throat. When I answered, it sounded like a croak. "Fine."

"You okay?"

"Sure. Just fine. How about you?"

"Just finished cutting three lawns. My summer business."

"Sounds hot."

"It is, but not in a cool way." He laughed.

"Hot, temperature-wise, not hot as in something fun to do," I explained, my face growing warm. How obvious could it be that I had no experience talking to a boy? "Th-that's what I meant," I stammered. "Hot out today."

"Hot every day in Atlanta in the summer."

Just shoot me, I thought. Why couldn't I say something cute or clever? "Um—can I do anything for you?" Now I sounded like I was helping out an inn guest.

"I was thinking I'd like for us to do something together."

My heart was hammering in my chest. "Like what?"

"Burger and a movie tomorrow? Or tonight. If you don't have plans."

Only helping Mom with our weekly cookout for guests. "Tomorrow would be better."

"Okay, then, I'll slide by around five? We can eat and grab an evening show."

"I'd like that."

He gave me his cell number, and after we hung up I went to my room and fell on my bed, kicking and exalting like a football player who'd just made the winning touchdown. I had a date! Me, Arabeth Thompson. And the guy was gorgeous. I hopped up, went to my dresser, and looked in the mirror. My face smiled back. Involuntarily my eyebrow arched, my mouth transformed into a pout, and my green eyes seemed to turn blue. I yelped and jumped back from my image. When I looked in the mirror again, my face looked like normal boring me. But I was shaken. For one brief moment I had looked like . . . like *her*. Impossible. I told myself that I'd studied the scrapbook too many times and had been thrown off balance by Wyatt's call.

I grabbed the book and shoved it under my bed. I didn't look in my mirror and quickly left my room.

"Absolutely not," Mom said. "You're too young to date."

"I am not!" I cried. "He's a really cool guy."

"I don't care if he's the Prince of Wales. You're not dating when you're fifteen."

We were in the kitchen, preparing for the evening cookout. Fortunately all our guests were out of the house for the afternoon, so I could yell. I stamped my foot. "You don't even know him!"

Mom gave me a smirk. "Point taken."

I'd walked into a trap.

She asked, "How did you meet him anyway?"

"He—Wyatt—came to visit with Kassey, that friend of Elowyn's." I had told Mom all about meeting Kassey and the coincidence of me and Elowyn liking the same flavor ice cream. I'd never told her about the other odd happenings surrounding my heart donor, though.

"Okay, so he's a friend of Kassey's. That's nice."

"The three of us talked and he liked me. He asked me out." I didn't tell her about Wyatt being Elowyn's former boyfriend. Too much information for Mom at the moment.

"And when was I going to meet him? On your way out the door?"

My brain was ticking through answers. He'd said I could call if I needed to change plans. "I can get him to come over. Maybe tonight."

She stopped shaping hamburger patties and sighed. "I'd like to meet him, but you're not dating him. And not tonight."

"That's so unfair!"

"I'm sure you think so." She dropped the burger onto a tray and faced me. "It's not just me . . . I promised your father."

That stopped me cold. "When? Promised him what?"

"Before he went off," she said.

I knew she was saying, ". . . the *last* time he went off."

She continued. "Before he left, he asked me to make sure you didn't wear makeup until you were at least fourteen, and that I wouldn't let you start dating until you were sixteen."

He'd missed two of my birthdays before he'd left for Afghanistan because he'd been on special assignment with the army, and now he'd never share my birthday again. Still, I didn't want to give up my argument. "I'll be sixteen in October."

"Months from now," she said.

"Wyatt will have forgotten all about me by then."

She held up her hand. "I told your father we were in agreement. At that time, neither of us were sure you'd *live* till you were sixteen. You were so sick and we were scared for you."

Invoking the memory of my father was something she rarely did, so I knew she was serious about my dating future. "I hadn't *wanted* to wear makeup until after my transplant," I said stubbornly. "Who ever saw me except family and the homebound teacher?"

"So it was a nonissue. This isn't."

"But no boy's ever asked me out before."

"A good thing. You'd have just heard the word *no* a little sooner." She turned back to her hamburgers. "Invite him over for tomorrow night. You can have our living room all to yourselves. I'll move up my baking schedule and stay out of your way all evening."

I'd set myself up for her solution since I'd volunteered to have him drop by. "He'll think I'm a baby."

"You're my baby," she said. "Now grab that head

of lettuce and those tomatoes and start getting the condiment platter together."

Still angry, I did as I was told. The kitchen was quiet except for the sound of Mom shaping burgers and my knife slicing through a ripe red tomato. I threw her a sideways glance and wondered why she and Dad would have taken the time to talk about me wearing makeup and dating when I was just a little girl. Thinking about my dad saddened me. I missed him, and I wouldn't be seeing him again. Not in this life.

I rehearsed what I would say to Wyatt, how I'd act breezy and casual. "Mom nixed me going out tomorrow night. How about you coming over here?" I was determined not to allow this opportunity to slip away. Now that I knew the truth about when I could actually date, how could I be sure that I'd ever be asked out again? And Wyatt was so cool. I couldn't let him get away. So how to date him without going out? Mom and Dad had dictated my future years ago and I was stuck with it. Maybe. If I—

The house phone rang, interrupting my thoughts. I jumped.

"Grab it," Mom called. "I'm elbow deep in hamburger meat."

I picked up the receiver, hoping it was Wyatt saving me from the trauma of calling him.

"Hi," a woman's voice said cheerfully. "Is this Arabeth?"

"Yes."

"This is Terri Eden. I've been thinking . . . I'd love to treat you and your mother to tea at the Ritz-Carlton. Do you think you can meet me there this Sunday?"

· 21 ·

Kassey

I got a job. In the months after Elowyn died, Wyatt and I had been pretty tight. Now he was busy with his lawn customers, his buddies, and yes, with Arabeth too, which was an adjustment for me. Plus I'd promised Mom I'd be responsible for my car, and gas was expensive, so a job seemed like the logical thing to pursue.

I landed one in a nursery—the kind that nurtures flowers, not kids. I liked it because I could be outside catching sun rays *and* get paid. I also joined a summer volleyball league at the Y—a good thing, because I could take out my feelings about life being unfair on the court and sometimes on the competition. In one game I spiked a ball hard over the net, catching a girl on the other side smack in the face and making her nose bleed. My bad.

Around July Fourth, I grew really bored. People, including Wyatt, were out of town. The Y was sponsoring a picnic, and so was Mom's office, but I didn't want to go to either one. In a fit of pure and utter boredom, I called Arabeth. She'd called me a few times earlier that summer and invited me over, but I'd always told her I was 'busy.' Now a day with her beat my alternatives. "Maybe we can catch the fireworks at Stone Mountain," I suggested over the phone. "Or at Six Flags."

"Really? You want me to go with you?" She sounded more excited than the situation warranted.

"Do you want to?"

"Absolutely! You'll save me from an evening with my family."

The inn was having a cookout when I arrived, and the food grilling on the barbecue smelled delicious. I met Arabeth's mother, her aunt Vivian and her uncle Theo, assorted cousins, and several inn guests who'd decided to hang around rather than brave holiday fireworks traffic.

"Don't leave. We can watch the show over in that direction," Aunt Viv said, pointing toward the sky over the backyard trees. "We'll eat home-churned ice cream and avoid the crowds."

Her idea sounded good to me. I'd forgotten about the crowds and traffic when I'd asked Arabeth to hit the road with me. "That okay with you?" I asked her.

She agreed, but looked disappointed.

"We'll blitz the mall next week," I said, to make it up to her. I liked her family, but I understood about wanting to shed them. Elowyn had always wanted to lose hers and I thought they were easy to be around.

"That would be fun," Arabeth told me, brightening.

As it grew darker, her mother asked, "Where are the sparklers we bought?"

"My room," Arabeth said. "I'll get them."

I tagged along behind her. When we entered her bedroom, I almost fell over. It resembled a French countryside, with sunny yellow walls and a wallpaper mural of fields of lavender. "What's this?" I asked, flabbergasted by the decor. "Where are we?"

"France," she said, crossing to a desk with a weathered farmhouse finish.

"You love France?"

"Not until after my transplant." She picked up a sack and turned toward me. "Another one of those weird things I was telling you about the first time we met. While I was in the hospital recovering, Mom and Aunt Viv redecorated my room, but it was what I requested. I just woke up yearning for a change and French country was all I wanted." She stared at me, then said knowingly, "It was Elowyn's choice too, wasn't it?"

"Totally. She was crazy about the whole country

of France. Went so far as to tell me she would marry a Frenchman and live in France someday."

"Well, I don't plan to marry a Frenchman," she said with a smile. "I escaped that craving."

I made my way around the room, studying the furniture, bedcover, and pillows. It really reminded me of Elowyn's old room. I guess French country-style decor was France no matter who did the decorating.

I stopped at a wooden chair with an oddly shaped saddle thrown over it. "This doesn't look like it came from France."

"It's a camel saddle, and it came from Afghanistan," said Arabeth.

"How did you end up with it?" I asked.

"It was a present from my father."

I thought back to the people I'd met that evening. There was no Mr. Thompson, so I figured Arabeth was just another girl with a broken family. Maybe her dad had left for better reasons than mine. "You own a camel?" I went for humor.

She shook her head. "Dad was in the army. A good soldier. He died in Afghanistan, killed by a roadside bomb."

A shiver shot up my spine. I'd never known anyone in the military. War was something only on TV news shows. "Gee . . . sorry. I wasn't trying to be nosey."

"It's history," she said, hugging the crinkled sack

against her body. "I miss him. I'm sorry he never knew about my transplant. It would have made him really happy."

We went outside. It had grown darker. Fireflies blinked in the night air. "Natural fireworks," I said, hoping to make her more cheerful. I hadn't meant to bring her down.

"I'll pass those out," her mother said, taking the sack. Everybody got two sparklers.

Arabeth said, "Let me show you something else. Something I'm sure Elowyn didn't have."

I followed her to the very back of the yard, to a small wooden house too big for a dog, but just right for small children. It was too dark to see it well, but I could tell it had an opening for a door and a window complete with small shutters.

Arabeth ducked inside. "It's a scrunch," she said, "but come on in."

I ducked into the doorway and joined her in the tight quarters.

"My dad made this for me when I was eight years old. He loved carpentry and was really good at it. I used to spend hours in here. My heart couldn't take the strain of playing, so this was my make-believe world. In here, I wasn't sick and I had a million friends, all wanting to come into my magic playhouse."

"It's pretty neat," I told her.

"Do you really think so?"

"I do." I slid down a wall, curling my knees tight to my chest. I held out one of my sparklers. "Got a match?"

She was hunched over hugging her knees too, but she fished a book of matches out of her shorts pocket. "Here you go."

I lit my sparkler and watched it ignite.

"It's the cool variety," she told me. "The barrel's hot, but not the sparks, so you won't get burned."

I tested the theory by capturing a few of the starry sparks. She was right. In the sizzle of light, I saw that her eyes looked large and unguarded. It didn't take a genius to realize how lonely she had been as a kid.

She touched her sparkler to mine and we watched as it caught, throwing sparks everywhere.

"You must have had a great dad," I said.

"Don't you?" she asked.

My sparkler came to the end of its life. "Not so much. He and Mom are divorced and he's been out of my life for a zillion years."

"Is that a zillion like in dog years?"

I laughed. I was beginning to really like her and I didn't think she was so creepy anymore just because she had some strange links to Elowyn. I liked her because she was honest and because she knew what it felt like to lose someone she loved.

"Hey, Arabeth and Kassey! The fireworks are starting," her mother called.

We crawled out of the house and looked up just as a burst of gold showered the dark sky and rained downward. A rocket boomed in the sky and I saw Arabeth cover her ears.

"I like to see fireworks, but I don't like the noise they make," she said.

"It's loud, all right."

We watched the sky fill with colors.

"It makes me think of Dad and the bomb that blew him up. I hope he didn't have time to feel any pain."

I had wondered the same thing about Elowyn. Had she seen the tree coming at her? Had she felt the air bag smash against her? Had she felt her head snap and hit the side window? Had she hurt before she died? I shuddered, struggling not to get teary as I sat on the grass watching fireworks beside the girl who sheltered my best friend's heart.

· 22 ·

Arabeth

My summer filled up with people paying attention to me. Not just family and doctors, but the new group made up of Wyatt, Kassey, and the Edens. Wyatt's attention was what interested me the most, of course. I had been scared that Mom's ban on me dating would be a turnoff for him, but he surprised me by shrugging it off. He came over a few times a week. I was nervous at first. Nothing to do but sit on the front-porch swing and talk, or watch DVDs, or sit in the backyard around the picnic table or on the Adirondack chairs. At first I apologized for the lack of excitement.

"Not a problem," he said. "Nothing wrong with hanging around. I like your backyard. It's pretty out here."

"Yard service," I confessed. "The place was a mess when we bought it, a real jungle." Mom's gardens were thick with blooming flowers and trimmed shrubs. The air was heavy with the scent of honeysuckle on vines and roses. We were outside eating fresh coconut cake at the picnic table. I pointed to one bed where a newly planted stand of lavender plants was growing—something I had wanted when I first came home from the hospital. "Kassey said that Elowyn liked everything French. Do you?"

"We were taking French and she loved to write me notes and text me in French, but I didn't like reading them. Give me English." He turned toward me. "You into French?"

I shook my head. "My room's decorated in French country, though."

He looked startled. "So was El's room."

"That's what Kassey told me." I explained how I woke up from my transplant with this odd craving for French decor. "It's bothered me for a long time—you know, this 'out of Arabeth's life experiences and into Elowyn's' I've been having ever since the transplant."

"It's freaky, all right."

I had a question for him, but felt self-conscious asking it.

"What?" he asked, sensing my mood.

"Do you . . ." I took a deep breath. "Do I remind you of her?"

He gave me a long thoughtful look. "Sometimes," he said.

His answer made my stomach knot. I didn't have the guts to ask "how?" Instead I asked, "What was she like?"

"Bubbly. Outgoing. People liked her."

"So she was perfect?"

He shook his head. "Hardly. She had a wild temper. I should know because she aimed it at me a lot."

I did a quick self-evaluation. Blowing up wasn't my style, and that realization made me feel better. I made a note to be calm and cheerful around him.

"Maybe we can figure it out," he said, out of the blue.

"Figure what out?"

"Why El's haunting you."

A chill ran up my spine. "I don't believe in ghosts," I said.

"Well, something's going on," he said.

"I keep thinking it will stop," I told him. "You know . . . if enough time passes."

He shrugged. "She was persistent too. Stubborn. Like a dog with a bone."

His words made me shiver. In the quiet of the summer night, all I wanted was for Elowyn to step out of my life and leave me alone.

After our first get-together at the Buckhead Ritz-Carlton, Terri started calling to chat and even began stopping by the inn. She surprised Mom and me by giving me a few of Elowyn's books. "I kept a box of her favorites," Terri said. "I donated most to charity, but I thought you might enjoy having her best-loved titles even though they're a little dog-eared."

I didn't know what to say.

"That's nice of you," Mom said for me. "Dog-eared just proves how much a book's adored."

"Thanks," I said.

Terri surprised us further when she came and booked a week's vacation at the inn for her and Matt. Mom was out grocery shopping, so I showed her the rooms and took the reservation.

Curious, I asked, "Why do you want to stay in Atlanta? You live here."

"Who has time to explore their own city? I mean, look at all the nice things to see and do in and around Atlanta. And a change of locale will be nice too." She smiled. "Plus, your mother's cooking must be a real treat."

Our inn had been written up a week before as a

top spot in the area and Mom's cooking had been praised. I returned Terri's smile. "I'm her sous-chef. No one brags on how nicely the vegetables are cut."

Terri laughed and squeezed my hand. "Arabeth, you're so funny."

I was pleased I could make her laugh. "You're all set for the last week in July for the Dolley Madison room." Mom had named the inn's rooms after famous early American women.

"Good." Terri took the paperwork. "So will you be here that week?"

"Sure, Mom needs my help because summer's so busy. I'll be hauling bags all week. At your service."

"Excellent. Having you around will make it more fun."

I watched her leave and wondered how in the world my presence could possibly add to her enjoyment.

I liked hanging around Kassey best of all. It had been a long time, since Monica, that I'd had a real friend. Being sick wasn't a way to collect them. Plus we'd moved and then I'd had the transplant and then I'd never clicked with anyone at Athena. It wasn't as if Kassey and I were real close, but she was smart and nice and said funny things that made me laugh.

When she wasn't working, we hit the mall together

and went to the movies and hiked a few walking trails. "I need to keep fit," she told me. "Volleyball and all."

"It helps me too," I said. We were on a greenway not too far from the inn. The day was hot, the air still and heavy. Leaves on the trees overhead dangled limp and dry. "I think about all the days I couldn't walk," I added. "Days I was on oxygen and could hardly breathe. Without the heart transplant, I'd be dead by now."

She slowed and looked at me. "That true?"

"I could smell the breath of the Grim Reaper."

She chuckled. "Don't joke about that."

I was trying to make my plight sound less desperate and pathetic. "I don't think about the bad times very much. I mean, I feel so good now, it's no fun remembering how bad it used to be."

She seemed lost for words, so I said, "Now don't feel sorry for me. I saw a lot of television and read a lot of books. Do you know I can quote whole pages of *Jane Eyre*?"

"I had to read it in eighth grade, but I could never get into it. Elowyn did, though." She grimaced. "I didn't mean to say that. Heck, tons of girls like *Jane Eyre*."

Suddenly the heat seemed oppressive. "We had a lot in common," I said. "I wonder why? I never knew her and yet she . . . she's influencing my life."

"I know about the ice cream and the French-decorated bedroom. Is there more?"

"When I was writing an essay for admission into Athena, I wrote the whole thing with my left hand . . . hundreds of words."

Kassey stopped in the middle of the trail and stared at me. "Your *left* hand?"

"It was automatic. I didn't even know it until the headmistress said something about it. I'm not left-handed. But I'll bet Elowyn was."

Kassey nodded. "That's what made her so valuable on the volleyball court. Opponents never saw her spikes coming."

I sighed. "I've never been able to write left-handed since that day. Not once."

Kassey looked sympathetic. "I don't know what to tell you." She looked up at the sky. The sun had vanished and the air smelled of sulphur. Kassey took my elbow. "We'd better hurry. A thunderstorm's coming."

Sure enough, the sky was darkening and a breeze was stirring the leaves. My mood darkened with the gathering clouds. Was I ever going to be free of Elowyn Eden?

"You know what we need to do?" Kassey asked, turning her voice cheerful and bright.

"Tell me."

"We need to spend a day at the Six Flags water park. Would you like to do that?"

I could have hugged her. "I'd love it."

The rain came, soaking us. We jogged back toward the parking lot and Kassey's car. She cracked jokes all the way and we sloshed in the rain puddles and giggled like two little kids.

· 23 ·

Arabeth

It was my job to help Mom serve breakfast and dinner to the inn's guests. I was also responsible for clearing dishes and silverware from the big farm table and loading the dishwasher after meals. I was carrying out platters of scrambled eggs and bacon from the kitchen when a woman called, "Arabeth, good morning."

Terri and Matt sat on the far side of the long table. "Hey," I said, giving them my brightest smile. It was Monday, so our weekend guests had gone, replaced by four couples who were staying for the week.

"Can you believe July's almost over?" Terri asked. Her smile beamed.

I set down the platters. "Welcome," I said.

Matt had been reading the newspaper, but he peered over the top at me. His blue eyes softened. "Good morning, Miss Arabeth."

"Are you two going exploring today?" I asked.

Terri glanced at Matt. "That's what we'd like to talk to your mother about."

"We have tons of sightseeing brochures at the front desk," I said. Mom kept the brochures well stocked. When guests asked for suggestions of places to see and explore, there were plenty of options to choose from.

"We have an agenda," Terri said. "We're heading to the new aquarium. Ever been there?"

I shook my head. "Not yet." The Atlanta aquarium was renowned and had been written up in all the travel magazines Mom bought.

Terri smiled broadly. "Can we talk to you and your mom in the kitchen?"

"I have to get the rest of the food. Come with me."

She followed me into the kitchen, where Mom was busy heaping her homemade cinnamon rolls into baskets. "Hi," she said, surprised to see Terri. She handed me two baskets. "I thought you'd gone back to bed," Mom grumbled at me.

"My fault," Terri said. "I was holding her up talking to her."

"Now!" Mom said, giving me a nudge toward the door. "While they're still warm."

I delivered the baskets, checked the juice and coffee pitchers on the table, and returned to the kitchen to refill them. Terri was talking to Mom, who was nodding, but she didn't look gloriously happy.

Mom turned to me. "The Edens want to know if you can go with them to the aquarium today."

"If your mother can spare you," Terri added in a conciliatory tone.

"Can I?" A day of doing something fun seemed great to me—like a reprieve from a work detail and wearing the orange jumpsuit.

"Monday's wash day," Mom said.

I was responsible for gathering the towels and doing the wash. My hopes took a nosedive.

"We can pick another day for the aquarium if that's more feasible," Terri said. "Matt and I would really like you to come with us."

Mom's lips pressed together. I knew she wasn't thrilled about a last-minute change of plans, but on the other hand, these were the people who'd donated their daughter's heart to me. "I'll call your aunt Vivian and see if she'll come over and pitch in," Mom said. "Your cousins are at church camp this week, so it's possible."

. . .

Terri and Matt made me feel like a princess all day long. Their car was plush, the nicest car I'd ever ridden in, and Terri bubbled over with conversation during the drive to the aquarium. We parked, and I watched Matt drape three cameras around his neck. I must have looked awed because he laughed and said, "I'm an amateur photographer. This one's digital video, this one's digital and small for grab shots, and this one uses plain old-fashioned film. I have a darkroom for developing film at the house."

"It's been his hobby for over a year," Terri said. "Ever since—" She stopped abruptly. Her expression darkened, then in a flash turned sunny. "Never mind. He loves photography, and I compile scrapbooks of our travels. We're the perfect couple." She hooked her arm through his.

The awkward moment passed and we went inside the building. We saw every exhibit, with Matt snapping photos of everything that moved. We only stopped long enough for lunch in the aquarium restaurant. "Pick whatever you want," Matt said, motioning to my menu.

Dining out wasn't something I did very much, but the menu choices were simple, so I chose a hamburger.

"You young people always get burgers," Matt said, leaving me to wonder if that was what Elowyn would have chosen too.

"Are you eager to begin school?" Terri asked me.

"Maybe not *eager*, but I've always liked school."

"Where do you attend?"

I took a bite out of my burger and told her about my scholarship offer to Athena, but also of how much I wanted to attend Roswell High.

"No contest," Terri said, picking at her salad. "Athena's the best. You must be very gifted. It's a wonderful opportunity."

"That's what Mom says too, but I really want to be in a regular school."

"Boys?" she asked knowingly.

"Wait until college," Matt said. "Better selection."

"That's where we met," Terri said.

"I rest my case."

They laughed at the joke between them. Terri turned to me. "Really, Arabeth, if you have a shot at graduating from Athena, take it." She dropped her gaze. "Listen to me . . . lecturing you. Sorry."

"That's okay," I said, not wanting to dampen her spirits.

"We wanted Elowyn to go to Athena, but she absolutely refused," Terri said. "She could be stubborn."

Matt reached over and took her hand. "We need a picture." He hopped up from the table and took several shots. I felt self-conscious, but it was making him happy, so I just smiled and leaned into Terri. She slid her arm around my shoulders and we mugged for the camera.

"You have fun?" Mom asked when we were alone later that night.

"I had a ball. They're really great people." I was on the sofa, surrounded by a silver dolphin, a plush killer whale, and an octopus, all thrust on me by Matt in the aquarium shop. "To remember our day together," he'd told me. I picked up the remote, ready to surf the Monday-night lineup.

"They certainly bought you a lot of stuff."

I glanced up and saw an edgy look cross Mom's face. I went on the defensive. "I tried to say no, but they insisted. It didn't seem like it was any big deal." She pressed her lips together. "Is it a big deal?" I asked, suddenly unsure of her mood.

"I'm just not sure you should encourage them."

"What do you mean?"

"They shouldn't be spending their money on you."

"Do you want me to give this stuff back? I will if you want me to."

She pinched the ridge between her nose and eyebrows. "No, no. It's okay. I shouldn't have brought it up. I'm happy you had a fun day."

I shrugged and returned my attention to the remote. Sometimes Mom could act a little strange. I mean, why would she object to a few stuffed animals from the Edens? I planned to put them on bookcases in my room and forget about them. What possible harm could it cause for me to own them?

· 24 ·

Kassey

I worked overtime at the nursery so that full-timers could take vacations, so it was August before Arabeth and I could hit the Six Flags water park. I picked her up early on a Friday and we headed off, trying to beat the crowds because the water park is very popular on hot Atlanta summer days. We found a place on the artificial beach of creamy white sand, spread out our towels, and slathered each other with sunscreen.

"I burn like a basted turkey," Arabeth said. "I'll bet you tan."

"I do." I didn't say, *Elowyn had to be careful too.* "I'll keep checking you so you don't fry," I said.

Arabeth flopped onto her back. "I turn often . . . like a chicken on a rotisserie," she said.

I giggled. I had started the summer not knowing

what to think of her, but I had grown to like her. Even though she was younger, she wasn't insufferable like many fifteen-year-old girls I knew at school. She had depth and sensitivity, and yes, she reminded me of Elowyn, all the time. Her own personality spilled out and gave me glimpses of a girl who'd spent hours alone all those years she was sick.

"I brought a couple of books," she said.

"I brought magazines," I said. "May as well check out the clothes I can't afford to buy for back-to-school."

She raised up on her elbow. "Don't you love those dopey features showing you how to get this mucho-dollar look for just a few bucks?"

"Yeah. As if I've got time to chase down outfits on the cheap. I hit the discount store and find my entire wardrobe in less than a day."

The smell of chlorine and the feel of warm sun was making me sleepy. Voices of yelling kids kept me from drifting off. My mind floated back to other summers when Elowyn and I had set up residency at her clubhouse pool and to the boys we'd tried to impress. Nostalgia hit me in waves.

"Did I tell you that Terri and Matt spent last week at our inn?" Arabeth said.

This news roused me. "Really?"

"They treated me pretty special."

I raised up. "How so?"

"They took me to the aquarium one whole day. Another afternoon I went to the Imax theater with them for a 3-D flick. Awesome."

The information pricked me like a sharp pin. "Why did they come to the inn?"

She shrugged. "They said it was for a vacation. I mean, who takes a vacation down the highway from where they live? I'll bet they can go anywhere they want. Like Europe. Or a cruise."

Images of other summers flashed past me. I could have told Arabeth about the vacations I'd taken with the Edens and Elowyn, but why? It would make me sad and probably not add anything to her day. I thought back to times Elowyn and I had spent with her parents. The Edens had treated me to gifts and meals, to many of the things they gave to Elowyn just because I was her best friend. "They're pretty nice people," I said casually.

"What was she like?" Arabeth asked. "You know, why were you two friends?"

I sat up, wrapped my arms around my knees and rested my chin on them. She'd asked an honest question, and I figured it was time to discuss Elowyn and satisfy Arabeth's curiosity. "She was kind and generous. She gave me clothes when it wasn't my birthday, even a key to her car before I got my license. And the key chain I carry—it's from Tiffany's."

Her eyes widened. "Nice present. Did you ever drive her car?"

"Never got a chance." I'd tossed the key into my desk drawer after her accident. I couldn't part with it although the car was long gone.

"Did you think she was perfect?"

I smiled. "She had a temper and when it went off, get out of her way."

"Wyatt said the same thing."

Wyatt. Hearing his name twisted my insides. "You still seeing him?"

"He comes over. Mom won't let me date, so we hang around the inn."

My first thought was "good," my second was wishful thinking about him and me not hanging out any longer. We hardly saw one another this summer. I missed his company, not just because we had Elowyn in common, but because I missed being around him. "That doesn't sound too bad," I finally said.

"I keep thinking he'll get bored and disappear."

I thought, *He never vanished on Elowyn.*

"You have a boyfriend?" Arabeth asked.

I stretched out my legs, watched kids riding the artificial waves from the wave machine. The sun sparkled off the blue water. "No," I answered honestly. "But my mom's dating. Some guy from her office. Nice, but nerdy."

"My mom hasn't dated since Dad . . . well, you know."

"It's embarrassing," I said. "I mean, my mom's got a guy and I don't."

"What do you suppose old people like them do?"

"They eat out."

"Do you think they, you know . . ."

We giggled together. This was exactly how Elowyn would have reacted, a smart comeback and then we'd laugh.

"Are we friends?" Arabeth picked lint off her towel.

Her question surprised me. "Sure."

"So friends can tell each other things and not expect it to be spread around, can't they?"

I hadn't imagined Arabeth holding secrets. "That's one definition of a friend."

She glanced around, although no one could have overheard us above the shrieks and shouts of the kids at the pool. "Wyatt and I sneaked off together one night. I know I shouldn't have. Mom was wiped out and had gone to bed early, so I called Wyatt and he met me out by my playhouse. We went through the bushes to where he'd parked his car one street over."

Her confession wasn't doing anything to relieve the knot in my insides. "Where did you go?" I made my voice as light as possible.

"He—he took me somewhere special. He said he

hadn't been there in years, but thought I'd like seeing it." She leaned in closer. "He took me to a place behind the airport on a dark road, and we parked. He spread a blanket on the hood of his car and we watched the planes take off. One came zooming right over where we were parked and shook the whole car with the sound of its engines. It was awesome."

I felt nauseous.

She dipped her head, picked at more lint on her towel where there was none. "And he . . . he kissed me right there under the stars."

· 25 ·

Kassey

I never let on to Arabeth how angry I was about Wyatt's taking her to his "special place." I stuffed my anger and faked having fun toasting in the sun, but as soon as I dropped her off, I hurried home, showered and changed, and drove straight to Wyatt's. His car was gone, so I parked in front of his house and waited. And I seethed. Not since the day I'd attacked him on my front-porch steps had I been so angry. And this time I was hurt too. He had kissed Arabeth. Just like he'd kissed me.

I'd been parked for about thirty minutes when he drove up, pulling a small trailer with his lawn mowers and other equipment. I met him on his front lawn.

"Kassey, what're you doing here?"

"We need to talk." Amazing how I could keep so calm when all I wanted to do was scratch out his eyes.

"Can I clean up first?"

"Whatever."

Inside his house, I sat on the sofa watching his twelve-year-old brother play a video game. His parents weren't home and I was glad because I knew I was going to yell. Wyatt emerged from the shower in clean clothes, rubbing his hair with a towel. He smelled like mint soap.

"My room," he said.

His brother never looked up. Wyatt's room was a mess, heaped with clothes and paper plates and soda cans. "Excuse the dump. I shovel it out once a week," he said, sweeping clutter off his bed for me to sit.

I didn't sit.

"Okay," he said, tossing the towel in a heap. "What's the problem?"

Facing him, I started to shake with pent-up fury, but I kept my voice steely. "I spent the day with Arabeth at the Six Flags water park."

"Okay."

"She told me, Wyatt. She told me how you took her out behind the airport and watched the planes take off. And that you kissed her."

His face reddened. "It was a spur-of-the-moment thing."

"Oh, please. You planned it."

He ignored my dig. "What's your point?"

"Is that the way you operate? Take girls to count planes and stars so you can hit on them?"

"It wasn't that way," he snapped. "I feel connected to El out there."

I almost exploded. "So connected that you have to kiss every girl you take?"

"Knock it off, Kassey. You don't know what I feel."

I knew what *I* was feeling—angry, guilty, betrayed.

"Why do you care who I take out there anyway?"

"*You* were Elowyn's guy. *You* belonged to her. *You* loved her." I didn't add, *And you made me think I was special.* But I thought how true that was.

"She's gone."

True enough, but I wasn't going to let him off so easily. "You're going to hurt Arabeth. You're going to break her heart."

"She's good-looking and I like her, but it's not just about her."

"Meaning?" I crossed my arms.

"I shouldn't have to tell you how she reminds me of Elowyn. You know what I'm saying. It's uncanny sometimes. She does or says something that makes it seem like El's in the room with me. Her expressions remind me. Her gestures. I look and listen for El when I'm with her."

I didn't look for these things with Arabeth like he did, but I recognized them when it happened. Arabeth would be herself, then, like quicksilver, she'd morph into a clone of Elowyn. "She isn't Elowyn," I said, gritting my teeth.

His eyes misted. "I know."

His show of emotion ramped down my anger. I hadn't expected it.

He sat slumped, staring at his hands. When he looked up, he said, "I want to show you something."

He rose, went to his dresser, and picked up his cell phone. He spent a minute scrolling through it with his thumbs, then handed it to me. "I've never shown this to another living soul."

I took the phone, glanced down at a text message dated the year before, the night Elowyn died. It read:

I hate u wyatt * hate hate hate * u said u love me
u don't. . . .

"Is that all?"

"The last message she ever sent. I think she was texting when she crashed."

I thought about the phone call I'd gotten from her that night. She'd been sobbing hard. Hadn't I also wondered if she'd been talking to me when she wrecked? Maybe it hadn't been a dropped call, but instead what had contributed to her accident.

Wyatt's shoulders sagged. "Do you know what it feels like thinking I caused her accident?"

Of course I did. "The rain caused it," I said. "The cops said it was the rain and a slick road and a tree." I sat beside him on the bed, all my anger spent. Pain and guilt seeped from his pores. There was nothing I could say to make it go away inside either of us.

I kept to myself after that. Wyatt and I gave one another a wide berth and I told Arabeth I was working long hours. It wasn't fair to her, but I didn't care. It bothered me knowing she was with Wyatt on long summer nights. I couldn't wait for school to start. I'd be a senior and I could bury myself in classes and volleyball. I'd been voted team captain again at the end of last season and I was ready to smash any opponent that came our way.

I kept seeing Elowyn's last text message to Wyatt in my head. Of course, she hadn't hated him. As the official go-between, I knew she loved him. And that had been their problem all along. They loved each other, but couldn't keep it together.

. . .

Days later I was hauling new flats of mums in a wagon at work when my cell vibrated in my pocket. I fished it out, saw Wyatt's name and number in the display. This was a surprise. I answered, not knowing what to expect. I said, "Hi."

He said, "Arabeth collapsed. They've taken her to the hospital."

part three

· 26 ·

Arabeth

I walk in a field under a blue-colored sky, the day so brilliantly bright that the landscape stands out in relief. I'm in a field of lavender, the scent sweet and heady. I've been transported, as if an alien spaceship has snatched me up and flown me away. I remember standing on my front porch. I remember a heavy weight on my chest, a staggering weight that I can't shake off. I hear Wyatt say, "Arabeth! What's the matter?"

And I wake up in paradise. I am alone, but I'm not afraid. Nothing matters except this place, the beauty surrounding me. The lavender waves in a breeze, not hot, not cold, just steady. The lovely tiny flowers rub against me and the scent sticks to my skin. I wonder where I am and why I'm here. I look for Mom. It isn't like her to let me go away by myself.

In the distance I see a line of trees along the edge of the field. A man emerges from the woods and walks toward me. I stop, raise my hand to shield my eyes, squint to bring him into focus in the blinding light of the sun. He's dressed in camouflage, the colors of desert sand and iron-stained earth. He wears a helmet and sand-colored boots. He carries a rifle, and there's a sidearm strapped around his thigh.

My heart beats faster. I can't see the man's face clearly, but I know his stance, I know how he holds his body and squares his shoulders. I know my father.

My heartbeat accelerates. I run toward him waving, screaming, "Daddy! Daddy!" He waves cheerfully. I run and run, but I make no progress. He halts, comes no closer.

I cry, "Dad, help me."

He watches, begins to gesture frantically for me to stop. He points for me to go back. I hear a voice inside my head say, "Arabeth, go home."

"I want to be with you, Daddy."

"Not yet," the inside-my-head voice says. "Go back."

I stop running, bend over to catch my breath. Suddenly I'm very tired, very sleepy.

I straighten in time to see my father step back into the woods and disappear like a vapor.

The field fades and blackness descends.

I begin to cry.

Mom calls me out of the darkness.

I struggle to open my eyes. My brain feels like it's swimming in mud, thick and gooey, sucking me down.

She holds my hand. "Wake up, baby. Please wake up."

My chest feels weighted. An oxygen mask covers my nose and mouth. I break through to the surface and see Mom's face hovering over mine. She's wearing a mask and gown. Just like in the days after I first received my transplant and I was in isolation, the days when even common germs were a life-ending threat. I groan.

"Thank God! Oh, thank God!" she says.

I want to speak.

"Don't," she says. "Just rest for now."

I ignore her. "What . . . ?"

"You passed out."

"Rejection?" I manage to mouth my biggest fear.

She nods. "But you're being treated. You'll be all right."

I'd better be. I can't become an invalid again. I won't.

"Rest," she says, patting my shoulder. "Time for questions later."

When later comes, I learn that I had "died." Clinical death is different from biological death. Often, with clinical death, the docs can bring you back to life. They put paddles on your chest, zap your heart with an electric charge, give you IV meds. You wake up. I woke up. Now I'm scared. I never expected my heart—Elowyn's heart—to fail me.

I grow strong enough to tell Mom, "I saw Daddy, standing in a field."

Her face goes pale. "You did?"

"He was dressed like a soldier. And he was perfect, Mom. No marks, no blood on him. I wanted to go to him. I wanted him to hold me."

"Did he?"

"He told me to come to him and I tried. Then he told me to go back, so I did. You believe me, don't you? About Daddy?"

Her eyes fill with tears. She smooths my hair. "Of course I believe you. I'm glad he sent you home. I'm glad you came back to me."

Dr. Chastain came to see me, carrying my medical file, already as thick as a phone book. "How are you feeling, Arabeth?"

"Fuzzy. A little numb."

He nodded. "It was touch and go for you."

The unvarnished truth. I winced. "Why . . . what happened to me?"

"You had a rejection episode."

"How?" This was a nightmare. I couldn't reject.

"You took something that set off the process."

"I did?" I tried to recall what I'd been doing before the pain hit me, before I passed out. I'd been with Wyatt. My mind stopped at this juncture. Did I have a seizure? Had I totally grossed him out? "I—I was with a friend," I told the doctor. "We were talking on the front porch."

"Had you taken something?"

Mom's brows knitted over this question. She was beside my bed listening to the doctor. "Are you asking her if she took illegal drugs?" She sounded insulted on my behalf.

"I would never do drugs," I said, tears brimming in my eyes. "I would never hurt my heart."

"We found a common cold remedy in your system."

That hit me like a train. I'd been feeling like I was coming down with a cold and I hadn't wanted to be all snuffly and sneezy around Wyatt. I'd taken some over-the-counter cold medication without even thinking.

"I told you mixing medications is dangerous and that you should not take anything unless I approve it.

The drugs you're on to safeguard your heart can cause unintended consequences. You could have died."

I was speechless. Without thinking, I'd done this to myself.

"I—I never thought to throw away . . . ," Mam began.

"You shouldn't have to," Dr. Chastain said. "This will be something that you'll have to guard against all your life, Arabeth."

I wished I could have slid under the sheet and disappeared. "I'll be more careful."

He squeezed my arm. "I'll move you out of isolation tomorrow, but I want you in the hospital for a few more days for observation."

"School's starting in two weeks," Mom told him. "Can she go?"

That idea hadn't crossed my mind. I panicked. I couldn't stand to return to a homebound program.

"Let's see how she does," the doctor said. "If she continues to improve, I don't see why not."

After he left, I looked at Mom. "I'm sorry. I'd forgotten about the medicine. I feel so good, and sometimes . . . sometimes I forget I've ever been sick."

She looked grim. "You have to always remember. I can't stand the thought of losing you."

"I'll be all right, Mom. I want to live a long, long time."

She rubbed her forehead. "You have a line of people wanting to see you."

"I do?"

"Aunt Viv and her family. Kassey. Wyatt." She took a breath. "And Terri and Matt Eden."

· 27 ·

Kassey

You don't know what you've got until it's gone—or as in the case of Arabeth, until it's almost gone. The day Wyatt called and told me what had happened, I freaked out. I trashed my room, throwing clothes, pillows, even a lamp—good news, it didn't break. I screamed, cried, pounded the walls. I couldn't believe this was happening all over again. I couldn't believe I was losing my best friend, Elowyn, for a second time.

Mom was working so she missed my meltdown, and I cleaned up before she got home. I told her about Arabeth the moment she walked through the door. "Oh, no," she said, tossing her purse and keys on the kitchen countertop. "Will she be all right?"

"I'm going to the hospital to check on her."

"Do you need me to come with you?"

A year and a half ago I had needed her with me, but not this time. "I'll call you when I know something."

She kissed me. "Be careful."

Arabeth was in isolation, so I couldn't get in to see her, and I was surprised to run into Terri in the waiting room. She looked pale and anxious. She put her arms around me. "Kassey, this is so horrible."

"How is she?"

"Alive. They brought her back in the ER. You know . . . with the paddles."

"Wyatt told me she wasn't breathing when the EMTs first came to the house. That her lips were blue and . . . and . . ." I couldn't finish.

"Wyatt was with her?"

I glanced around, but he wasn't in the waiting area. "Yes, he was. How did you find out about what happened?"

"I had called the inn, just to chat with her, ask her if I could take her to lunch and go shopping. We had such a nice time when we stayed the week. Anyway, a woman, I think her aunt, answered the phone and told me. She'd just returned from the ER to take care of inn guests."

"Have you talked to anyone since you've been here?"

"Her mother. She told me Arabeth was resting

now." Terri paused. "And that the doctors say she had a rejection episode and it caused her heart to fibrillate and . . . and . . . stop."

Terri's face looked tortured. I understood because I was feeling the same sense of déjà vu. We were reliving Elowyn's last days, the roller-coaster ride between hope and despair. "She's going to make it," I said shakily. "Elowyn won't let her die."

Terri buried her face in her hands. "I miss her so much," she whispered. "Every day. Sometimes I forget. I see something I know she'd like, and I get excited and say, 'El, look at this.' But of course, she can't. Just knowing that her heart lives on inside Arabeth has kept me sane. It's my living link to her."

A knot wedged in my throat. Wasn't this what all of us—me, Wyatt, the Edens—had felt? As long as Arabeth was alive, so was Elowyn. And the freaky coincidences when Arabeth mirrored Elowyn's characteristics and personality kept us bound to the idea. I cleared my throat. "Where's Matt?"

"He came and stayed awhile, until we knew Arabeth was alive. He told me he couldn't do this again. He can't just sit and wait. It's too painful."

"Arabeth will be all right," I said. "She will."

Once she was moved to a private room, I could visit Arabeth. She appeared to be all right, except that her face looked puffy. "Steroids," she explained. "I'm back on massive doses of the antirejection drugs. I hope to look normal by the time school starts."

"You decide which school you're going to?" I knew about her wish to attend Roswell High. After the day we'd spent at the water park, I knew many things about her. I was feeling ashamed that I hadn't kept in closer contact since that day.

"I'm going back to Athena. Why not? I know the place, the teachers, what's expected of me. And it's free this year."

"But you told me you wanted to be around boys."

"I changed my mind."

I would have asked why, but just then Wyatt entered the room. He stopped. "Kassey, you're here."

I felt out of place and seeing him bumped up my heart rate. I hadn't seen him since the day of our fight or talked to him since the night he'd called from the hospital. "I—I can come back."

"No," he and Arabeth said in unison.

Her face had reddened and she looked uncomfortable. Not at all like a girl excited about being with her boyfriend that I had expected to see. "It's okay," she said. "I can have two visitors at a time."

Wyatt said, "Stay. I have something to show you both." He carried a file folder and walked it over to

Arabeth's tray table, which was pushed across her bed. He picked up her water jug and set it on another table and opened the file folder, fanning out several pieces of printed paper.

"And this is . . . ?" I asked, baffled.

"My research. I spent hours surfing the Web last night. It took me a while to figure out how to search, but I eventually came up with the term 'cellular memory.'"

He looked pleased with himself and as if we should have caught right on to what he was talking about. "Okay," I said. "I'll bite. What's 'cellular memory'?"

"It's what's been happening to Arabeth. The episodes of being like Elowyn." He stared at Arabeth. "You know, the weird things you do that are her and not you."

I picked up a piece of paper and read out loud. "'Sometimes a phenomenon is reported by transplant patients of having memories or of doing actions that belonged to their donor.'"

Wyatt said, "It's most common with heart transplants."

I got goose bumps. Arabeth said, "Go on."

Wyatt shuffled papers. "I printed out case histories. Here's one where a recipient got a guy's heart and she woke up craving a beer and a cig. She'd never drunk or smoked. And here's one where a man got a woman's heart and now he buys things in the color pink and the special perfume she always used."

That hit close to home because Arabeth wore the same fragrance as Elowyn had worn.

"I guess it's good you got a girl's heart," I said to her. "You might have wanted to take up football or fishing."

She smiled, but sobered quickly. "Do you think this could be what's happening to me?"

"Seems logical," Wyatt said. "One recipient reported that she saw bright lights and felt heat on her skin, and it turned out that her donor had died of smoke inhalation in a fire."

"I had a dream once," Arabeth said. "I dreamed I was driving in rain, really bad rain, and I—I was crying. And the car skidded and there was a tree right in front of me."

You could have heard a pin drop in the room. She glanced at both of us. "I only had it once," she added, as if in defense.

Wyatt tucked the paperwork into the file folder and closed it. "I thought you should know about cellular memory," he said quietly.

"Why didn't my doctor mention it?"

"Real science thinks it's a load of—" He stopped himself. "You know, that it's not possible."

"It's real to me," Arabeth said.

"And to me," I said. "Sometimes it's been like Elowyn is in the room with me."

Wyatt nodded in agreement. "Not your fault, Arabeth. Sometimes you *are* her."

She studied us both. "Does your research tell how a recipient can lose a donor? How she can get those cell memories to leave her alone?"

"The syndrome isn't medically accepted. I don't know how you can lose the sense of her you have. I wish I did, but there's no research on that," Wyatt said.

"So I just have to put up with her invading my mind forever?"

I hadn't thought of it like that. I hadn't considered how it made Arabeth feel to be in someone's else's thoughts with no warning. Of what it must be like to see her life through someone else's eyes. "Maybe it'll go away in time, as you get more strength and your life keeps changing," I said hopefully.

Arabeth pushed back into her pillows and stared up at the ceiling. "I know she was a wonderful person. I know you both loved her. I know you're both here because I remind you of her. I get it. But just remember . . . I'm Arabeth Thompson. This is who I'll always be. It's who I always want to be."

· 28 ·

Arabeth

They didn't know I was awake, and they didn't know I could overhear them while they stood on the other side of my hospital room talking. Their whispers were soft at first, but grew louder as they discussed me.

At first Mom's voice held just a hint of irritation. "Terri, you don't have to hang around this hospital day in and day out. Arabeth's doing fine. Her doctor is telling me he'll send her home in a couple of days."

Terri said, "I know, but I'm just worried about her."

"Why?" Mom asked. "I told you she's doing fine."

"She almost died."

"That isn't—" Mom stopped herself. "Before she got the heart, she almost died several times. She was a very sick girl."

"It must have been terrible for you. As her mother, I mean."

"And that's the point. I *am* her mother." Mom's words were loaded.

Terri didn't answer right away, but finally she stammered, "I—I know . . . I—I'm not trying to be her mother. . . ."

"Listen, we will always be grateful for the gift you gave us. It was an act of untold generosity and I don't know how else to say thank you."

I lay on my side rigid in the bed, fully awake. I peeked open one eye and made out Mom and Terri in the gloom of the fading evening light coming through the window behind them.

"Just seeing her getting better is thanks enough."

"You say that, but it isn't enough, is it?" Mom said.

"I like being around her." Terri's words came haltingly. "She . . . she reminds me so much of Elowyn. She even acts like her."

"But she isn't Elowyn. She isn't your daughter."

Terri's head jerked up. "I know. Do you think I don't know that?"

Mom massaged her forehead, the place between

her eyes that she always rubs when she's stressed out. "Sometimes you don't act like you know it. You take her places. You buy her things. You treat her as if she's yours."

My heart hammered and the blip quickened on the monitor I was hooked up to. I cursed the machine. Both of their heads turned toward me and I shut my eye, afraid they might catch me listening in. The interruption settled Mom and Terri and the tension between them lessened.

"I like being around her. Me and Matt both. We like her company. It's comforting. It fills up the holes inside us. I miss my Elowyn so much." Terri's voice cracked.

I almost sat up in bed and clamped my hands over my ears. I wished I could split myself in two. I wished I could be a daughter to both my mother and Terri. I ventured another peek. Mom had reached over and taken Terri's hand.

"Terri, go home. Please. I know you hurt, but neither Arabeth nor I can fix it."

Terri turned to stare at me. "If . . . if she has another problem . . . will you call me?"

"I really don't think that's a good idea. It won't help you break off this attachment."

Terri looked stricken and glared at Mom. She pulled away and rushed out the door without another word. Mom slumped against the wall. I shut my eyes because it hurt too much to see her sadness and to feel Terri's raw pain. My heart squeezed. Medical science or not, I knew Elowyn was hurting too.

The brightest spot during my hospital stay came from Kassey's visits. I needed a girlfriend, and she was the closest thing I had going. Yes, she'd been Elowyn's best friend, but that didn't bother me. Whenever she came into the room, she lifted my mood. Sometimes I even believed that Elowyn was drawing us closer together, especially if there was any truth to Wyatt's cellular memory information.

"They ever letting you out of this place?" Kassey was sitting in my room, her feet propped up on the side of my bed. She'd brought a few videos for us to watch.

"Maybe tomorrow. I've been whining to my doc for days. School starts next week and I'm going even if I have to drag this stupid monitor with me."

She grinned. "That's a threat. I'm sure your doc is worried about you leaving with hospital property."

"He better be," I groused.

"Has Terri sneaked in for a visit since she and your mom had it out?"

Naturally I'd told Kassey everything. "No. Mom scared her off."

"I feel sorry for her. I mean, Elowyn was hers and Matt's whole world."

"I like them, and they were nice to me."

"I like them too," Kassey said. "Matt was crazy about Elowyn. She could twist him around her finger and get most anything she wanted. I used to envy her . . . I mean, with my dad gone and all."

"My dad was a pushover too. I remember when he built my playhouse—the day we'd come home from a doctor's visit when the doctor had said I needed to stop going to the playground. That it was getting too strenuous for me. I loved the playground on the army base. I cried and cried."

Kassey looked sympathetic.

"Dad showed me a magazine with all kinds of playhouse plans. I picked the one I liked best and we even went to the lumberyard together to buy the wood. I picked out the colors for it—lime green and pink—and he painted it after he'd built it. Mom bought me a little table and chairs to put inside and it was my favorite place to be in the whole world."

"I like it too. A little small now, though, as I remember from Fourth of July."

I smiled. "It was a friend magnet. At least for a while. But everybody grows up."

"Do you know your eyes shine when you talk about your father?"

Kassey's observation made me blush. "Sorry."

"No, it's cool. Elowyn had a great dad. You had a great dad. That's outstanding."

I sipped some water, hesitated for a second before I said, "I saw Dad the day I collapsed. I saw him as plain as day."

"You mean you dreamed you saw him."

I shook my head. "He was as real as you are."

She looked skeptical. "Tell me about it."

I'd only told Mom my story. I didn't want Kassey to think I was totally nuts, but the experience had been so real—plus it was my experience, not Elowyn's. "I was walking in a field of flowers, in sunlight. It was the most beautiful day I've ever seen. The colors were supercharged, really intense," I said. "And Dad came out from behind a line of trees. . . ."

· 29 ·

Kassey

I couldn't get Arabeth's experience with her dead father out of my mind. I'd asked her, "Was it one of those out-of-body experiences? You know, like you read about and hear about on TV?"

"I don't know."

"I mean, you had died, hadn't you? Do you think you went to this place while you were dead? Before they zapped you back?"

She'd shrugged. "I had no sense of time. One minute I was on my porch talking to Wyatt, then my chest hurt, then I was in this beautiful place, and my father found me. I wanted to stay, and at first he wanted me to stay. But then he told me to go back, so I did. Next thing I knew I was in the hospital and Mom was begging me to stay with her."

Yet it was more than the story itself that fascinated me. It was what she said right before I left to come home. I was digging in my purse for my car keys when she said, "You're very lucky, Kassey."

I glanced up, followed the lead wires partially covered by her hospital gown reaching over to the heart monitor. "I know."

"Not about this," she said, pointing to the monitor. "You're lucky because your father's still alive. I'd give anything if mine was. I got to see my father. That was the best part . . . seeing him alive and well and perfectly whole. You know, a roadside bomb destroys a soldier, so I couldn't see him at his burial."

I had nothing to say.

"He was so happy when he saw me across that field of flowers," she added, flashing a radiant smile.

Even now, in the privacy of my room, I got chills remembering Arabeth's words and the expression on her face. *I was lucky.* I'd never thought so. My dad left Mom and me and we'd gone on without him. He'd come back into our lives. He wanted me to care about him, and I'd said no way. He'd said he was sorry. He sent us money. He'd made our lives better since first contact. Mom had forgiven him. Why hadn't I?

I turned on the TV. I turned the TV off. I picked up a teen magazine. I put it down. I made chocolate pudding and filled dessert dishes. I cleaned the kitchen.

Nothing calmed my restlessness. Finally, I sat down at Mom's computer and called up my father's e-mail address. Staring at the blank screen, I didn't know how to begin.

Dear Dad <delete>
Father <delete>
Dear person who walked away <delete> <delete>
Steve <delete>

Finally, I just started typing. The message was short, but I was certain he would respond.

Dad . . . it's me, Kassey. I'll be a senior this school year, so I guess it's about time we got to know each other. You go first.

I was buying school supplies in a superstore and ran smack into Wyatt—and a pretty blond girl who was holding his hand. She looked familiar, but I couldn't place her. Wyatt said, "This is Cindi."

"I was JV cheerleading last year," Cindi said. "You played awesome volleyball."

Now I remembered her.

"I've moved up to varsity this year."

If I was supposed to be impressed, I wasn't. "Cheer on," I said.

She gave me a quizzical look. Her gaze shifted and she waved to someone behind me. "Yoo-hoo! Allison!" I turned to see a girl two aisles over. "I'll be back in a jiff," Cindi said, and took off toward Allison.

Wyatt shifted from foot to foot.

"New girlfriend?" I asked.

"Now don't go chewing my butt, Kassey. I like Cindi and . . . and it's been a long time since—well, you know."

I held up my hand. "It's all right. You should move on."

He looked as if he was waiting for a punch line, but I had none to give him.

"What about Arabeth?" I asked.

He jammed his hands into the back pockets of his jeans. "You were right. She's too young for me."

"Lame," I chided, recalling that I'd once told him that.

He stared at a spot above my head. "I like her. She's nice." His gaze connected with mine. "She scared the crap out of me when she went down on the porch. I broke her fall, but she was out. Her face was turning blue and she was gasping for air. I thought I was going to have a heart attack waiting for the EMTs to arrive. If her aunt hadn't been there and given her CPR—" He stopped short. "I can't do this again. I can't get involved with a girl like Arabeth."

I knew what he meant: He couldn't get attached to a girl who was a few heartbeats away from a permanent checkout. "Does she know?"

"Know what?"

I gestured over my shoulder with my thumb to the effervescent Cindi.

He shrugged. "I don't know."

"You haven't told Arabeth?"

He looked embarrassed. "Don't know what to say."

"You go see her and break it off. It's a courtesy."

"I can text her," he offered.

"Coward. No e-mails either."

"Can't you tell her for me?"

I rolled my eyes. "Do I have to smack you again?"

He grinned. "Management will never let you in the store again if you do."

I returned his smile. For the first time in a long time, I felt comfortable around him, like in the days when the boundary lines between us were clearly drawn. It had been Elowyn who had brought us together; it was the loss of Elowyn that had kept us together. Trying to relive our experiences with Elowyn had forced us apart and turned us into the odd couple. And it was Arabeth and her uncanny links to Elowyn that had messed with our heads.

Cindi came bounding up, linked her arm through Wyatt's. "I can't wait to tell you what Allison told me."

I backed away. "Look, I've got to go. I'll see you at school."

Wyatt said, "Sure thing."

Cindi said, "I'll be your best cheerleader when you play volleyball."

"Can't wait," I said.

I walked toward the cashier, clutching the basket holding my back-to-school supplies. I checked out, and walked quickly to the exit. When the soft swish of the automatic door closed behind me, I knew another door was closing too.

· 30 ·

Arabeth

I was going home from the hospital. Crisis over.
Mom was on her way to come get me. She'd called to
say she was stuck in traffic. "The road's at a stand-
still," she said, sounding exasperated.

"It's all right," I told her. "I'll get packed up, then
I'll wait in the room until you show up. You don't
want me to miss my favorite soap, do you?"

That made her laugh because I wasn't a fan of any
soap operas.

I was putting my stuff in a suitcase when I heard
a man clear his throat from behind me. I turned to see
Matt Eden framed in the doorway. "Matt! What a
nice surprise." My heart accelerated because I hadn't
seen either him or Terri since Mom's discussion with
Terri. Surely Terri had told him what Mom had said.

"Hello, Arabeth. I hope you don't mind me dropping by."

"No, no. It's good to see you," I said, feeling flustered.

"So you're blowing this pop stand, are you?"

It took me a minute to catch on to his meaning. When I did, I said, "Oh, you mean I'm getting out of here. Yes, Mom's on her way."

"I'm happy you're going home. Terri and I want you to be happy and well."

"Um—I appreciate that." I paused. "How is Terri?"

"She's fine." He held out a gift bag. "She wanted me to give you this."

I took the bag. "You don't have to—"

"Just a little something to remember us by."

"Are you leaving?"

"In a way. I want you to know we won't be hanging around you like we have been."

My face got hot and I knew I was red-faced. "Mom didn't mean—"

"Shhhh," he said. "That wasn't meant to hurt your feelings. It was just a clarification of our place in your life."

"You have an important place in my life."

"You're kind to say so." His southern drawl was soothing. He nodded at the bag in my hand. "You going to open that?"

"Oh, sure." I pulled at the bag, lifted out a small scrapbook with a lavender leather cover. "For me?"

"None other. Terri put it together."

I sat on the bed, opened the book. In lovely gold-lettered calligraphy were the words: HEART 2 HEART. HANDMADE FOR ARABETH THOMPSON. A photograph of me laughing was centered on the page. I turned page after page only to see myself at the aquarium, at the inn serving food, smiling in many different settings. The photos were beautiful, and I was dumbstruck. "How did you take all these? I remember posing for some, but the others . . ."

He looked pleased. "Mostly when you weren't looking. But you're a pretty subject, so it wasn't difficult to get grab shots."

Terri had arranged the photos on colorful background pages, with cleverly placed decals and symbols to highlight the settings.

"I—I don't know what to say."

"Just knowing you like the book is thanks enough."

"I love it!"

"Terri will be happy to know that."

One page held a shot of Mom and me leaning over the picnic table working a puzzle in deep concentration, our foreheads almost touching. In the background the haunting image of a soldier had been Photoshopped into the picture. On the last page were photos arranged in a circle. Terri and Matt; Mom and an old photo of my dad surrounding pictures of Elowyn and me. There we were, strangers who might have never met except for a heart transplant. I ran my fingers across the picture of my dad. "Where did you get this one?"

"I called your mother and asked for it."

"And she . . . she didn't mind?"

He grinned. "She was kind and generous. I knew Terri was way overinvolved with your life. I understood and your mother does too. You don't belong to us, Arabeth. You're not our child."

I nodded. "I feel close to you, though."

"We got off-track because sometimes . . . well, you say and do things that make Elowyn seem alive again. Not your fault. It's unnerving, though. One minute you're Arabeth, the next she seems to jump right out at us."

I didn't bring up Wyatt's cellular memory theory. It was best to let Terri and Matt cut the strings. "I'll be grateful forever to all of you."

He rocked back on his heels. "It would be nice if you'd contact us from time to time. Not regularly. Just now and again. Like when life milestones come up, such as graduation, getting married, things like that."

"I will."

He searched my face. Did he see Elowyn now?

I watched his eyes tear up. "You take care of yourself, Arabeth. You'll never be far from our thoughts."

My own eyes filled too. I turned my head. He backed out of the doorway. At the last second, I heard him whisper, "Goodbye, Sugar Plum."

And without hesitation, words spilled out of my mouth that I had not planned to say. Words that came in a voice clear and gentle, and different from mine. I said, "I love you, Daddy."

· 31 ·

Kassey

"I think she's gone and out of my life," Arabeth told me dramatically.

We were sitting at the picnic table on her back patio licking ice cream cones—not Chunky Monkey but mint chocolate fudge. The afternoon was hot and still. We were in our bathing suits, and a kiddie pool and a rotating sprinkler were waiting for us on the grass.

Of course, I knew instinctively she was talking about the reflection of Elowyn imprinted in her cells. "How do you know?"

"I just feel it. I'm my old self again. Boring ole me."

I grinned. "So what's it feel like to be you?"

She thought about that, then said, "Happy. Excited

about school starting. Are *you* happy? About school and volleyball, I mean."

I licked a dribble sliding down the side of my cone. "I am. It'll be good to get back on the courts. How about you? Any sports at Athena you can play?"

"I might go out for cross-country. My doctors tell me my heart is sound and I can run. It's been years since I've run hard."

Arabeth wore a one-piece tank suit, but I could see the top of her scar from her transplant. "You should think about volleyball."

She wrinkled her nose. "You're the superstar in that field."

We slurped in silence, licking quickly because the sun was melting the ice cream. She licked a trail off her hand. "Do you hear from Wyatt?" I asked.

"Not since I came home from the hospital. But it's okay. We were never meant to be a couple."

"How do you know?"

She gave up on the trail of liquid ice cream and let it run down her arm. "I could never be sure if he really liked me, Arabeth, or the parts of Elowyn he saw in me. I want a boyfriend who just wants Arabeth."

It made perfect sense. "I'm glad you weren't too attached to him."

"I liked him well enough." Her expression turned wistful, then brightened. "And I'll always be grateful because he gave me my first kiss. And now I can concentrate on finding someone to give me my second kiss. I'm over the 'what if we bump noses' trauma."

I laughed out loud. "That's one way to look at it."

We dumped our cone leftovers, rinsed off, and climbed into the pool. We were too big for it and our legs dangled over the edges, but the water was cooler than the air. I stirred the water with my hands. In the far back part of the yard, I considered the playhouse, draped with branches of hot pink crepe myrtle flowers. "News flash," I said.

Arabeth flipped pool water across her face and the droplets shimmered on her skin. "Go on."

"I've been e-mailing my father."

She sat up straighter. "You have?"

"I guess I've been mad at him long enough. Mom's forgiven him. I guess I should too."

"You should," Arabeth said. "Where is he? Will you see him anytime soon?"

"He's working in an engineering firm out west. I invited him to come for my graduation next May. Mom told me I've done the right thing and my dad was pumped about the invite." It sounded funny to my ears to be saying "my dad."

We lazed in the pool, letting the hot sun beat down on us. The sprinkler made a pass and rained water on us every few minutes.

"I want to ask you something," Arabeth said.

Her voice sounded timid. I opened one eye. "Okay, ask me."

She took a deep breath. "Mom's rented a cabin at Altoona Lake for Labor Day weekend. Aunt Viv and Uncle Theo will man the inn so she and I can get away."

I closed my eye. "Sounds like fun."

"Mom says she's going to sleep, read, and eat chocolate for three days. Not much fun for me."

I listened because Arabeth was leading up to something.

"She said . . . she told me I could invite a friend to stay with us. You know, so I won't be bored out of my skull. I was hoping you could come. It's sort of like a long sleepover. Just a short vacation, and we won't miss any school. I'll have a better time if I take a friend with me."

I turned my face toward her. Her expression was eager and her eyes questioning. My heart picked up its pace. A vacation. Just like the ones I went along on with Elowyn and her parents. I could have told that to Arabeth. But hadn't she told me she was free of Elowyn's influence? Didn't she believe she was her own person once more?

"You don't want to go. You probably have plans." Arabeth looked crestfallen. "That's okay. It was a long shot."

She started to rise, but I reached for her arm.

"Wait. I was going over my social calendar mentally, and guess what? Nothing!"

She eased back into the water. "Really?"

"Zilch. I'd like to come. Mom and I never take vacations."

A smile lit up her face. "I'll tell Mom. She likes you."

The sprinkler made another pass. The spray fell on us and the pool water. I watched the ripples spread. It was decided. We would go on vacation. Just Arabeth's mother, Arabeth, and me.

And the heart of Elowyn Eden.

Lurlene McDaniel began writing inspirational novels about teenagers facing life-altering situations when her son was diagnosed with juvenile diabetes. "I saw firsthand how chronic illness affects every aspect of a person's life," she has said. "I want kids to know that while people don't get to choose what life gives to them, they do get to choose how they respond."

Lurlene McDaniel's novels are hard-hitting and realistic, but also leave readers with inspiration and hope. Her books have received acclaim from readers, teachers, parents, and reviewers. Her bestselling novels include *Don't Die, My Love, I'll Be Seeing You, Till Death Do Us Part, Hit and Run,* and *Prey.*

Lurlene McDaniel lives in Chattanooga, Tennessee.